# SHORT SHORTS

"[The Howes] have devised the most original anthology since Randall Jarrell's *The Anchor Book of Stories* . . . I would give it to anybody."

—Walter Clemons,
*Newsweek*

"[These stories] are small only in measure. All contain social and psychological resonances that sound long after this remarkable book is closed."

—Stefan Kanfer,
*Time*

"Writers who do short shorts need to be especially bold. They stake everything on a stroke of inventiveness. Sometimes they have to be prepared to speak out directly, not so much in order to state a theme as to provide a jarring or complicating commentary. The voice of the writer brushes, so to say, against his flash of invention. And then, almost before it begins, the fiction is brought to a stark conclusion—abrupt, bleeding, exhausting. This conclusion need not complete the action, it has only to break off decisively."

—Irving Howe,
*from the Introduction*

# SHORT SHORTS

## An Anthology of the Shortest Stories

EDITED BY
IRVING HOWE AND
ILANA WIENER HOWE
with an Introduction by Irving Howe

BANTAM BOOKS
NEW YORK • TORONTO • LONDON • SYDNEY • AUCKLAND

*This edition contains the complete text
of the original hardcover edition.*
NOT ONE WORD HAS BEEN OMITTED.

SHORT SHORTS: AN ANTHOLOGY OF THE SHORTEST STORIES
*A Bantam Book*

*PUBLISHING HISTORY*
*First published in the U.K. in 1982 by Kudos & Godine, Publisher, Ltd.
David R. Godine, Publisher edition published June 1982.*

*(For copyright notices, see the Acknowledgments section on pages 197-200, which constitutes an extension of the copyright page.)*

*Bantam edition / December 1983*



ISBN 0-553-27440-6

*Published simultaneously in the United States and Canada*

---

**Bantam Books are published by Bantam Books, a division of Bantam Doubleday Dell Publishing Group, Inc. Its trademark, consisting of the words "Bantam Books" and the portrayal of a rooster, is Registered in U.S. Patent and Trademark Office and in other countries. Marca Registrada. Bantam Books, 1540 Broadway, New York, New York 10036.**

---

PRINTED IN THE UNITED STATES OF AMERICA

KR 14 13 12 11

# Table of Contents

*Part Two*

IRVING HOWE

# Introduction

LIKE OTHER GREAT EVENTS in history, this collection of short short stories (hereafter called short shorts) has its origin in family talk around the kitchen table.

One editor was reading "Swaddling Clothes," a marvelous story by the Japanese writer Mishima, and naturally enough urged the other editor also to read it. Which the other editor did and, of course, agreed: yes, a superb piece of work. There soon followed a conversation in which the two editors found themselves noticing that Mishima's story seemed different from the usual kind of short story. How so? It is fiercely condensed, almost like a lyric poem; it explodes in a burst of revelation or illumination; it confines itself to a single, overpowering incident; it bears symbolic weight. Struggling to define this story's distinctiveness, the two editors began to wonder: Were they talking about a separate literary genre, or subgenre, which might be called the short short? And if there is some good reason for talking about the short short, are there perhaps others, not as great as Mishima's but still worth gathering, that might be put together in "a little book"?

They set out to look; they found; and here is the little book. It's a book to be read for pleasure, first and foremost; and if you don't think that finally there is much difference between short stories and these short shorts, well, the editors won't burst into tears. But since they do maintain that there are significant differences, let's glance at these in the next few pages.

The one thing we can be sure of is that the short short is shorter than the short story. As an outer limit for the short short we'd suggest twenty-five hundred words. As the norm, fifteen hundred words. Who decreed this? No one; it's only a suggestion. But we think it makes sense. Our short shorts are indeed like most ordinary short stories, *only more so*—but that's just the point, *only more so* makes for important differences:

In the ordinary short story—say, between three and eight thousand words—there isn't much opportunity for the writer to develop character through an extensive action or in psychological depth. There isn't the space in which to show the changes, whether toward growth or decline, that occur in human beings across a span of time. Still, it's at least possible to *present* a character in the ordinary short story. We know quite a bit, for example, concerning O.E. Parker in Flannery O'Connor's "Parker's Back" and even more about Gabriel Conroy in James Joyce's longer story, "The Dead."

There can't be much development of action or theme in such stories, but at least there is some. By contrast, in the short short the very idea of character seems to lose its significance, seems in fact to drop out of sight. We see human figures in a momentary flash. We see them in fleeting profile. We see them in archetypal climaxes which define their mode of existence. Situation tends to replace character, representative condition to replace individuality.

Consider Ernest Hemingway's "A Clean, Well-Lighted Place." What do we know, or need to know, about the man who sits in the café piling up saucers? Next to nothing about his past, very little about his future. What we do know, unforgettably, is the wracking loneliness and lostness of his life in the present.

Or consider Octavio Paz's "The Blue Bouquet." We know almost nothing about the man threatened with the loss of his eyes, since the crux of the story is not biography but confrontation—that moment of danger in which the man finds himself, a moment such as any of us could experience. Faced with that danger, he loses whatever fragment of individuality he may have for us, and all that matters is the color of his eyes.

In both Hemingway's and Paz's miniature masterpieces, circumstance eclipses character, fate crowds out individuality, an extreme condition serves as emblem of the universal.

The usual short story cannot have a complex plot, but it often has a simple one resembling a chain with two or three links. The short short, however, doesn't as a rule have even that much—you don't speak of a chain when there's only one link. In Isaac Babel's "The Death of Dolgushov," Luigi Pirandello's "The Soft Touch of Grass," Varlam Shalamov's "In the Night" (to cite only three examples) there is the barest, briefest incident. And that's all—a flick of the eye, a quick response, from which we have to draw whatever pleasure or insight that we can.

Sometimes, as in Sholom Aleichem's "A Yom Kippur Scandal" and Grace Paley's "Wants," the short short appears to rest on nothing more than a fragile anecdote which the writer has managed to drape with a quantity of suggestion. A single incident, a mere anecdote—these form the spine of the short short.

Everything depends on intensity, one sweeping blow of perception. In the short short the writer gets no second chance. Either he strikes through at once or he's lost. And because it depends so heavily on this one sweeping blow, the short short often approaches the condition of a fable. When you read the two pieces by Tolstoy in this book, or I. L. Peretz's "If Not Higher," or Franz Kafka's "The

Hunter Gracchus," you feel these writers are intent upon "making a point"—but obliquely, not through mere statement. What they project is not the sort of impression of life we expect in most fiction, but something else: an impression of an *idea* of life. Or: a flicker in darkness, a slight cut of being. The shorter the piece of writing, the more abstract it may seem to us. In reading Paz's brilliant short short we feel we have brushed dangerously against the sheer arbitrariness of existence; in reading Peretz's, that we have been brought up against a moral reflection on the nature of goodness, though a reflection hard merely to state.

Could we say that the short short is to other kinds of fiction somewhat as the lyric is to other kinds of poetry? The lyric does not seek meaning through extension, it accepts the enigmas of confinement. It strives for a rapid unity of impression, an experience rendered in its wink of immediacy. And so too with the short short. Even in those, like Tolstoy's "Alyosha the Pot" and Giovanni Verga's "The Wolf," which cover a stretch of time in the lives of the portrayed figures, there is finally a strong impression of timelessness—as if to say, we don't need detail or extension, the whole thing comes to us in a flash, the fatality of Alyosha and the compulsiveness of "the Wolf."

Writers who do short shorts need to be especially bold. They stake everything on a stroke of inventiveness. Sometimes they have to be prepared to speak out directly, not so much in order to state a theme as to provide a jarring or complicating commentary. The voice of the writer brushes, so to say, against his flash of invention. And then, almost before it begins, the fiction is brought to a stark conclusion—abrupt, bleeding, exhausting. This conclusion need not complete the action; it has only to break it off decisively.

Here are a few examples of the writer speaking out directly. Paz: "The universe is a vast system of signs." Kafka in "First Sorrow": The trapeze artist's "social life was somewhat limited." Paula Fox: "We are starving here in our village. At last, we are at the center." Babel's cossack cries out, "You people with glasses have about as much pity for our kind as a cat for a mouse." Such sentences serve as devices of economy, oblique cues. Cryptic and enigmatic, they sometimes replace action, dialogue and commentary, for none of which, as it happens, the short short has much room.

There's often a brilliant overfocussing.

No one reading Jerome Weidman's masterful "My Father Sits in the Dark" is likely to forget its solitary image: the old man sitting there, alone in the kitchen, seemingly content to ruminate about his life or perhaps just stare into unresponsive space. It pierces the heart. It speaks to the human condition in some profound way. Yet we would have a hard time saying precisely in which way, for there is something mysterious about this image, communicating more than we can say about it. And much the same is true with regard to another of our short shorts, also dealing with a withdrawn father, João Guimaraes Rosa's "The Third Bank of the River," which yields an image equally haunting and inexhaustible. We might say, this wonderful short short has to do with the human need both to be away and keep in sight; but we know that barely begins to describe it.

Let's press ahead a little further by sketching out a few variations among short shorts:

ONE THRUST OF INCIDENT. (Examples: Paz, Mishima, Shalamov, Babel, W.C. Williams.) In these short shorts the time span is extremely brief, a few hours, maybe even a few minutes: Life is grasped in symbolic compression. One might say that these short shorts constitute epiphanies (climactic moments of high grace or realization) that have been torn out of their contexts. You have to supply the contexts yourself, since if the contexts were there, they'd no longer be short shorts.

LIFE ROLLED UP. (Examples: Tolstoy's "Alyosha the Pot," Verga's "The Wolf," D. H. Lawrence's "A Sick Collier.") In these you get the illusion of sustained narrative, since they deal with lives over an extended period of time; but actually these lives are so compressed into typicality and paradigm, the result seems very much like a single incident. Verga's "Wolf" cannot but repeat her passions, Tolstoy's Alyosha his passivity. Themes of obsession work especially well in this kind of short short.

SNAP-SHOT OR SINGLE FRAME. (Examples: García Márquez, Böll, Katherine Anne Porter.) In these we have no depicted event or incident, only an interior monologue or flow of memory. A voice speaks, as it were, into the air. A mind is revealed in cross-section—and the cut is rapid. One would guess that this is the hardest kind of short short to write: There are many pitfalls such as tiresome repetition, being locked into a single voice, etc.

LIKE A FABLE. (Examples: Kafka, Keller, von Kleist, Tolstoy's "Three Hermits.") Through its very concision, this kind of short short moves past realism. We are prodded into the fabulous, the strange, the spooky. To write this kind of fable-like short short, the writer needs a supreme self-confidence: The net of illusion can be cast only once.

When we read such fable-like miniatures, we are prompted to speculate about significance, teased into shadowy parallels or semi-allegories. There are also, however, some fables so beautifully complete (for instance Kafka's "First Sorrow") that we find ourselves entirely content with the portrayed surface and may even take a certain pleasure in refusing interpretation.

Enough. I leave to the reader to decide whether these remarks have established the claim that there are significant differences between short stories and short shorts. Divisions of genre serve a purpose somewhat like a scaffolding: useful as preliminaries but in the end to be discarded. And meanwhile, not another word—for what could be more absurd than a long long introduction to a book of short shorts?

IRVING HOWE

# Short Shorts

# Part One

LEO TOLSTOY

# The Three Hermits

## AN OLD LEGEND CURRENT IN THE VOLGA DISTRICT

And in praying use not vain repetitions as the Gentiles do: for they think that they shall be heard for their much speaking. Be not therefore like them; for your Father knoweth what things ye have need of, before ye ask Him.

*Matthew vi: 7,8.*

A BISHOP was sailing from Archangel to the Solovétsk Monastery, and on the same vessel were a number of pilgrims on their way to visit the shrines at that place. The voyage was a smooth one. The wind favorable and the weather fair. The pilgrims lay on deck, eating, or sat in groups talking to one another. The Bishop, too, came on deck, and as he was pacing up and down he noticed a group of men standing near the prow and listening to a fisherman, who was pointing to the sea and telling them something. The Bishop stopped, and looked in the direction in which the man was pointing. He could see nothing, however, but the sea glistening in the sunshine. He drew nearer to listen, but when the man saw him, he took off his cap and was silent. The rest of the people also took off their caps and bowed.

"Do not let me disturb you, friends," said the Bishop. "I came to hear what this good man was saying."

"The fisherman was telling us about the hermits," replied one, a tradesman, rather bolder than the rest.

"What hermits?" asked the Bishop, going to the side of the vessel and seating himself on a box. "Tell me about them. I should like to hear. What were you pointing at?"

"Why, that little island you can just see over there," answered the man, pointing to a spot ahead and a little to the right. "That is the island where the hermits live for the salvation of their souls."

"Where is the island?" asked the Bishop. "I see nothing."

"There, in the distance, if you will please look along my hand. Do you see that little cloud? Below it, and a bit to the left, there is just a faint streak. That is the island."

The Bishop looked carefully, but his unaccustomed eyes could make out nothing but the water shimmering in the sun.

"I cannot see it," he said. "But who are the hermits that live there?"

"They are holy men," answered the fisherman. "I had long heard tell of them, but never chanced to see them myself till the year before last."

And the fisherman related how once, when he was out fishing, he had been stranded at night upon that island, not knowing where he was. In the morning, as he wandered about the island, he came across an earth hut, and met an old man standing near it. Presently two others came out, and after having fed him and dried his things, they helped him mend his boat.

"And what are they like?" asked the Bishop.

"One is a small man and his back is bent. He wears a priest's cassock and is very old; he must be more than a hundred, I should say. He is so old that the white of his beard is taking a greenish tinge, but he is always smiling, and his face is as bright as an angel's from heaven. The second is taller, but he also is very old. He wears a tattered peasant coat. His beard is broad, and of a yellowish grey color. He is a strong man. Before I had time to help him, he turned my boat over as if it were only a pail. He too is kindly and cheerful. The third is tall, and has a beard as white as snow and reaching to his knees. He is stern, with overhanging eyebrows; and he wears nothing but a piece of matting tied round his waist."

"And did they speak to you?" asked the Bishop.

"For the most part they did everything in silence, and spoke but little even to one another. One of them would just give a glance, and the others would understand him. I asked the tallest whether they had lived there long. He frowned, and muttered something as if he were angry; but the oldest one took his hand and smiled, and then the tall one was quiet. The oldest one only said: 'Have mercy upon us,' and smiled."

While the fisherman was talking, the ship had drawn nearer to the island.

"There, now you can see it plainly, if your Lordship will please to look," said the tradesman, pointing with his hand.

The Bishop looked, and now he really saw a dark streak—which was the island. Having looked at it a while, he left the prow of the vessel, and going to the stern, asked the helmsman:

"What island is that?"

"That one," replied the man, "has no name. There are many such in this sea."

"Is it true that there are hermits who live there for the salvation of their souls?"

"So it is said, your Lordship, but I don't know if it's true. Fishermen say they have seen them; but of course they may only be spinning yarns."

"I should like to land on the island and see these men," said the Bishop. "How could I manage it?"

"The ship cannot get close to the island," replied the helmsman, "but you might be rowed there in a boat. You had better speak to the captain."

The captain was sent for and came.

"I should like to see these hermits," said the Bishop. "Could I not be rowed ashore?"

The captain tried to dissuade him.

"Of course it could be done," said he, "but we should lose much time. And if I might venture to say so to your Lordship, the old men are not worth your pains. I have heard say that they are foolish old fellows, who understand nothing, and never speak a word, any more than the fish in the sea."

"I wish to see them," said the Bishop, "and I will pay you for your trouble and loss of time. Please let me have a boat."

There was no help for it; so the order was given. The sailors trimmed the sails, the steersman put up the helm, and the ship's course was set for the island. A chair was placed at the prow for the Bishop, and he sat there, looking ahead. The passengers all collected at the prow, and gazed at the island. Those who had the sharpest eyes could presently make out the rocks on it, and then a mud hut was seen. At last one man saw the hermits themselves. The captain brought a telescope and, after looking through it, handed it to the Bishop.

"It's right enough. There are three men standing on the shore. There, a little to the right of that big rock."

The Bishop took the telescope, got it into position, and he saw the three men: a tall one, a shorter one, and one very small and bent, standing on the shore and holding each other by the hand.

The captain turned to the Bishop.

"The vessel can get no nearer in than this, your Lordship. If you wish to go ashore, we must ask you to go in the boat, while we anchor here."

The cable was quickly let out; the anchor cast, and the sails furled. There was a jerk, and the vessel shook. Then, a boat having been lowered, the oarsmen jumped in, and the Bishop descended the ladder and took his seat. The men pulled at their oars and the boat moved rapidly towards the island. When they came within a stone's throw, they saw three old men: a tall one with only a piece of matting tied round his waist, a shorter one in a tattered peasant coat, and a very old one bent with age and wearing an old cassock—all three standing hand in hand.

The oarsmen pulled in to the shore, and held on with the boathook while the Bishop got out.

The old men bowed to him, and he gave them his blessing, at which they bowed still lower. Then the Bishop began to speak to them.

"I have heard," he said, "that you, godly men, live here saving your own souls and praying to our Lord Christ for your fellow men. I, an unworthy servant of Christ, am called, by God's mercy, to keep and teach His flock. I wished to see you, servants of God, and to do what I can to teach you, also."

The old men looked at each other smiling, but remained silent.

"Tell me," said the Bishop, "what you are doing to save your souls, and how you serve God on this island."

The second hermit sighed, and looked at the oldest, the very ancient one. The latter smiled, and said:

"We do not know how to serve God. We only serve and support ourselves, servant of God."

"But how do you pray to God?" asked the Bishop.

"We pray in this way," replied the hermit. "Three are ye, three are we, have mercy upon us."

And when the old man said this, all three raised their eyes to heaven, and repeated:

"Three are ye, three are we, have mercy upon us!"

The Bishop smiled.

"You have evidently heard something about the Holy Trinity," said he. "But you do not pray aright. You have won my affection, godly men. I see you wish to please the Lord, but you do not know how to serve Him. That is not the way to pray; but listen to me, and I will teach you. I will teach you, not a way of my own, but the way in which God in the Holy Scriptures has commanded all men to pray to Him."

And the Bishop began explaining to the hermits

how God had revealed Himself to men; telling them of God the Father, and God the Son, and God the Holy Ghost.

"God the Son came down on earth," said he, "to save men, and this is how He taught us all to pray. Listen, and repeat after me: 'Our Father.' "

And the first old man repeated after him, "Our Father," and the second said, "Our Father," and the third said, "Our Father."

"Which art in heaven," continued the Bishop.

The first hermit repeated, "Which art in heaven," but the second blundered over the words, and the tall hermit could not say them properly. His hair had grown over his mouth so that he could not speak plainly. The very old hermit, having no teeth, also mumbled indistinctly.

The Bishop repeated the words again, and the old men repeated them after him. The Bishop sat down on a stone, and the old men stood before him, watching his mouth, and repeating the words as he uttered them. And all day long the Bishop labored, saying a word twenty, thirty, a hundred times over, and the old men repeated it after him. They blundered, and he corrected them, and made them begin again.

The Bishop did not leave off till he had taught them the whole of the Lord's Prayer so that they could not only repeat it after him, but could say it by themselves. The middle one was the first to know it, and to repeat the whole of it alone. The Bishop made him say it again and again, and at last the others could say it too.

It was getting dark and the moon was appearing over the water, before the Bishop rose to return to the vessel. When he took leave of the old men they all bowed down to the ground before him. He raised them, and kissed each of them, telling them to pray as he had taught them. Then he got into the boat and returned to the ship.

And as he sat in the boat and was rowed to the ship he could hear the three voices of the hermits loudly repeating the Lord's Prayer. As the boat drew near the vessel their voices could no longer be heard, but they could still be seen in the moonlight, standing as he had left them on the shore, the shortest in the middle, the tallest on the right, the middle one on the left. As soon as the Bishop had reached the vessel and got on board, the anchor was weighed and the sails unfurled. The wind filled them and the ship sailed away, and the Bishop took a seat in the stern and watched the island they had left. For a time he could still see the hermits, but presently they disappeared from sight, though the island was still visible. At last it too vanished, and only the sea was to be seen, rippling in the moonlight.

The pilgrims lay down to sleep, and all was quiet on deck. The Bishop did not wish to sleep, but sat alone at the stern, gazing at the sea where the island was no longer visible, and thinking of the good old men. He thought how pleased they had been to learn the Lord's Prayer; and he thanked God for having sent him to teach and help such godly men.

So the Bishop sat, thinking, and gazing at the sea where the island had disappeared. And the moonlight flickered before his eyes, sparkling, now here, now there, upon the waves. Suddenly he saw something white and shining, on the bright path which the moon cast across the sea. Was it a seagull, or the little gleaming sail of some small boat? The Bishop fixed his eyes on it, wondering.

"It must be a boat sailing after us," thought he, "but it is overtaking us very rapidly. It was far, far away a minute ago, but now it is much nearer. It cannot be a boat, for I can see no sail; but whatever it may be, it is following us and catching us up."

And he could not make out what it was. Not a boat, nor a bird, nor a fish! It was too large for a man, and besides a man could not be out there in the midst of the sea. The Bishop rose, and said to the helmsman:

"Look there, what is that, my friend? What is it?" the Bishop repeated, though he could now see plainly what it was—the three hermits running upon the water, all gleaming white, their grey beards shining, and approaching the ship as quickly as though it were not moving.

The steersman looked, and let go the helm in terror.

"Oh, Lord! The hermits are running after us on the water as though it were dry land!"

The passengers, hearing him, jumped up and crowded to the stern. They saw the hermits coming along hand in hand, and the two outer ones beckoning the ship to stop. All three were gliding along upon the water without moving their feet. Before the ship could be stopped, the hermits had reached it, and raising their heads, all three as with one voice, began to say:

"We have forgotten your teaching, servant of God. As long as we kept repeating it we remembered, but when we stopped saying it for a time, a word dropped out, and now it has all gone to pieces. We can remember nothing of it. Teach us again."

The Bishop crossed himself, and leaning over the ship's side, said:

"Your own prayer will reach the Lord, men of God. It is not for me to teach you. Pray for us sinners."

And the Bishop bowed low before the old men; and they turned and went back across the sea. And a light shone until daybreak on the spot where they were lost to sight.

*Translated by Louise and Aylmer Maude*

## LEO TOLSTOY

# Alyosha the Pot

ALYOSHA was a younger brother. He was nicknamed "the Pot," because once, when his mother sent him with a pot of milk for the deacon's wife, he stumbled and broke it. His mother thrashed him soundly, and the children in the village began to tease him, calling him "the Pot." Alyosha the Pot: and this is how he got his nickname.

Alyosha was a skinny little fellow, lop-eared—his ears stuck out like wings—and with a large nose. The children always teased him about this, too, saying "Alyosha has a nose like a gourd on a pole!"

There was a school in the village where Alyosha lived, but reading and writing and such did not come easy for him, and besides there was no time to learn. His older brother lived with a merchant in town, and Alyosha had begun helping his father when still a child. When he was only six years old, he was already watching over his family's cow and sheep with his younger sister in the common pasture. And long before he was grown, he had started taking care of their horses day and night. From his twelfth year he plowed and carted. He hardly had the strength for all these chores, but he did have a certain manner—he was always cheerful. When the children laughed at him, he fell silent or laughed himself. If his father cursed him, he stood quietly and listened. And when they finished and ignored him again, he smiled and went back to whatever task was before him.

When Alyosha was nineteen years old, his brother was taken into the army; and his father arranged for Alyosha to take his brother's place as a servant in the merchant's household. He was given his brother's old boots and his father's cap and coat and was taken into town. Alyosha was very pleased with his new clothes, but the merchant was quite dissatisfied with his appearance.

"I thought you would bring me a young man just like Semyon," said the merchant, looking Alyosha over carefully. "But you've brought me such a sniveller. What's he good for?"

"Ah, he can do anything—harness and drive anywhere you like. And he's a glutton for work. Only looks like a stick. He's really very wiry."

"That much is plain. Well, we shall see."

"And above all he's a meek one. Loves to work."

"Well, what can I do? Leave him."

And so Alyosha began to live with the merchant.

The merchant's family was not large. There were his wife, his old mother and three children. His older married son, who had only completed grammar school, was in business with his father. His other son, a studious sort, had been graduated from the high school and was for a time at the university, though he had been expelled and now lived at home. And there was a daughter, too, a young girl in the high school.

At first they did not like Alyosha. He was too much the peasant and was poorly dressed. He had no manners and addressed everyone familiarly as in the country. But soon they grew used to him. He was a better servant than his brother and was always very responsive. Whatever they set him to do he did willingly and quickly, moving from one task to another without stopping. And at the merchant's, just as at home, all the work was given to Alyosha. The more he did, the more everyone heaped upon him. The mistress of the household and her old mother-in-law, and the daughter, and the younger son, even the merchant's clerk and the cook—all sent him here and sent him there and ordered him to do everything that they could think of. The only thing that Alyosha ever heard was "Run do this, fellow," or "Alyosha, fix this up now," or "Did you forget, Alyosha? Look here, fellow, don't you forget!" And Alyosha ran, and fixed, and looked, and did not forget, and managed to do everything and smiled all the while.

Alyosha soon wore out his brother's boots, and the merchant scolded him sharply for walking about in tatters with his bare feet sticking out and ordered him to buy new boots in the market. These boots were truly new, and Alyosha was very happy with them; but his feet remained old all the same, and by evening they ached so from running that he got mad at them. Alyosha was afraid that when his father came to collect his wages, he would be very annoyed that the master had deducted the cost of the new boots from his pay.

In winter Alyosha got up before dawn, chopped firewood, swept out the courtyard, fed grain to the cow and the horses and watered them. Afterwards, he lit the stoves, cleaned the boots and coats of all the household, got out the samovars and polished them. Then, either the clerk called him into the shop to take out the wares or the cook ordered him to knead the dough and to wash the pans. And later he would be sent into town with a message, or to the school for the daughter, or to fetch lamp oil or something else for the master's old mother. "Where have you been loafing, you worthless thing?" one would say to him, and then another. Or among themselves they would say, "Why go yourself? Alyosha will run for you. Alyosha, Alyosha!" And Alyosha would run.

Alyosha always ate breakfast on the run and was seldom in time for dinner. The cook was always chiding him, because he never took meals with the others, but for all that she did feel sorry for him and always left him something hot for dinner and for supper.

Before and during holidays there was a lot more work for Alyosha, though he was happier during holidays, because then everyone gave him tips, not much, only about sixty kopeks usually; but it was his own money, which he could spend as he chose. He never laid eyes on his wages, for his father always came into town and took from the merchant Alyosha's pay, giving him only the rough edge of his tongue for wearing out his brother's boots too quickly. When he had saved two rubles altogether from tips, Alyosha bought on the cook's advice a red knitted sweater. When he put it on for the first time and looked down at himself, he was so surprised and delighted that he just stood in the kitchen gaping and gulping.

Alyosha said very little, and when he did speak, it was always to say something necessary abruptly and briefly. And when he was told to do something or other or was asked if he could do it, he always answered without the slightest hesitation, "I can do it." And he would immediately throw himself into the job and do it.

Alyosha did not know how to pray at all. His mother had once taught him the words, but he had forgot even as she spoke. Nonetheless, he did pray, morning and evening, but simply, just with his hands, crossing himself.

Thus Alyosha lived for a year and a half, and then, during the second half of the second year, the most unusual experience of his life occurred. This experience was his sudden discovery, to his complete amazement, that besides those relationships between people that arise from the need that one may have for another, there also exist other relationships that are completely different: not a relationship that a person has with another because that other is needed to clean boots, to run errands or to harness horses; but a relationship that a person has with another who is in no way necessary to him, simply because that other one wants to serve him and to be loving to him. And he discovered, too, that he, Alyosha, was just such a person. He realized all this through the cook Ustinja. Ustinja was an orphan, a young girl yet, and as hard a worker as Alyosha. She began to feel sorry for Alyosha, and Alyosha for the first time in his life felt that he himself, not his services, but he himself was needed by another person. When his mother had been kind to him or had felt sorry for him, he took no notice of it, because it seemed to him so natural a thing, just the same as if he felt sorry for himself. But suddenly he realized that Ustinja, though completely a stranger, felt sorry for him, too. She always left him a pot of kasha with butter, and when he ate, she sat with him, watching him with her chin propped upon her fist. And when he looked up at her and she smiled, he, too, smiled.

It was all so new and so strange that at first Alyosha was frightened. He felt that it disturbed his work, his serving, but he was nonetheless very happy. And when he happened to look down and notice his trousers, which Ustinja had mended for him, he would shake his head and smile. Often while he was working or running an errand, he would think of Ustinja and mutter warmly, "Ah, that Ustinja!" Ustinja helped him as best she could, and he helped her. She told him all about her life, how she had been orphaned when very young, how an old aunt had taken her in, how this aunt later sent her into town to work, how the merchant's son had tried stupidly to seduce her, and how she put him in his place. She loved to talk, and he found listening to her very pleasant. Among other things he heard that in town it often happened that peasant boys who came to serve in households would marry the cooks. And once she asked him if his parents would marry him off soon. He replied that he didn't know and that there was no one in his village whom he wanted.

"What, then, have you picked out someone else?" she asked.

"Yes. I'd take you. Will you?"

"O Pot, my Pot, how cunningly you put it to me!" she said, cuffing him playfully on the back with her ladle.

At Shrovetide Alyosha's old father came into town again to collect his son's wages. The merchant's wife had found out that Alyosha planned to marry Ustinja, and she was not at all pleased. "She will just get pregnant, and then what good will she be!" she complained to her husband.

The merchant counted out Alyosha's money to his father. "Well, is my boy doing all right by you?" asked the old man. "I told you he was a meek one, would do anything you say."

"Meek or no, he's done something stupid. He has got it into his head to marry the cook. And I will not keep married servants. It doesn't suit us."

"Eh, that little fool! What a fool! How can he think to do such a stupid thing! But don't worry over it. I'll make him forget all that nonsense."

The old man walked straight into the kitchen and sat down at the table to wait for his son. Alyosha was, as always, running an errand, but he soon came in all out of breath.

"Well, I thought you were a sensible fellow, but what nonsense you've thought up!" Alyosha's father greeted him.

"I've done nothing."

"What d'you mean nothing! You've decided to marry. I'll marry you when the time comes, and I'll marry you to whoever I want, not to some town slut."

The old man said a great deal more of the same sort. Alyosha stood quietly and sighed. When his father finished, he smiled.

"So I'll forget about it," he said.

"See that you do right now," the old man said curtly as he left.

When his father had gone and Alyosha remained alone with Ustinja, who had been standing behind the kitchen door listening while his father was talking, he said to her: "Our plan won't work out. Did you hear? He was furious, won't let us."

Ustinja began to cry quietly into her apron. Alyosha clucked his tongue and said, "How could I not obey him? Look, we must forget all about it."

In the evening, when the merchant's wife called him to close the shutters, she said to him, "Are you going to obey your father and forget all this nonsense about marrying?"

"Yes. Of course. I've forgot it," Alyosha said quickly, then smiled and immediately began weeping.

From that time Alyosha did not speak again to Ustinja about marriage and lived as he had before.

One morning during Lent the clerk sent Alyosha to clear the snow off the roof. He crawled up onto the roof, shovelled it clean and began to break up the frozen snow near the gutters when his feet slipped out from under him and he fell headlong with his shovel. As ill luck would have it, he fell not into the snow, but onto an entry-way with an iron railing. Ustinja ran up to him, followed by the merchant's daughter.

"Are you hurt, Alyosha?"

"Yes. But it's nothing. Nothing."

He wanted to get up, but he could not and just smiled. Others came and carried him down into the yard-keeper's lodge. An orderly from the hospital arrived, examined him and asked where he hurt. "It hurts all over," he replied. "But it's nothing. Nothing. Only the master will be annoyed. Must send word to Papa."

Alyosha lay abed for two full days, and then, on the third day, they sent for a priest.

"You're not going to die, are you?" asked Ustinja.

"Well, we don't all live forever. It must be some time," he answered quickly, as always. "Thank you, dear Ustinja, for feeling sorry for me. See, it's better they didn't let us marry, for nothing would have come of it. And now all is fine."

He prayed with the priest, but only with his hands

and with his heart. And in his heart he felt that if he was good here, if he obeyed and did not offend, then there all would be well.

He said little. He only asked for something to drink and smiled wonderingly. Then he seemed surprised at something, and stretched out and died.

*Translated by S.A. Carmack*

## HEINRICH VON KLEIST

# The Beggarwoman of Locarno

AT THE FOOT of the Alps, near Locarno in northern Italy, stood an ancient castle belonging to a Marquis, which today, coming down the St. Gotthard, one sees in ruins before one—a castle with great, high-ceilinged rooms, in one of which the mistress of the house one day spread a bed of straw out of pity for a sick old woman who had come begging to her door. When the Marquis returned from hunting, he happened to walk into this room, where he kept his shotgun, and irritably ordered the woman to get up out of the corner where she was lying and find herself a place behind the stove. The woman, as she rose, slipped with her crutch on the polished floor and fell, injuring her spine so seriously that it was only with an immense effort that she was able to get up again and cross the room as she had been bidden, but once behind the stove she collapsed, groaning and sighing, and died.

Several years later, when war and bad harvests had brought the Marquis into straitened circumstances, there appeared a Florentine knight who liked the castle's beautiful situation and offered to buy it. The Marquis, who was extremely eager to sell, told his wife to put the stranger up in the unoccupied room mentioned above, which was furnished very splendidly. But imagine the couple's dismay when the knight came downstairs, pale and shaken, in the middle of the night and swore the room was haunted: something invisible to the eye, he said, had got up from the corner with a rustling sound, as if from a bed of straw, quite audibly crossed the room with slow and feeble steps, and collapsed, groaning and sighing, behind the stove.

The Marquis, frightened without knowing why himself, laughed at the knight with forced heartiness, and offered to get up on the spot and pass the night with him in the room, if that would set his mind at rest. But the knight asked him to be good enough to let him spend the rest of the night in an armchair in the Marquis' bedroom, and when morning came he called for his coach, paid his respects, and left.

This incident, which created a great sensation, frightened away several prospective buyers, much to the Marquis' chagrin; and when, oddly and inexplicably, it began to be whispered even among his own people that a ghost walked the room at midnight, he decided to investigate the matter himself, so as to put an end, once and for all, to the rumors. At nightfall, accordingly, he had his bed made up in the room and waited, wide awake, for midnight to come. But imagine his dismay when, at the witching hour, he in fact heard the mysterious noise: it was as if someone got up from a heap of rustling straw, crossed the room, and collapsed, sighing and gasping, behind the stove. The next morning, when he came downstairs, the Marquise asked how his investigation had turned out; and when he looked around him apprehensively and, after bolting the door, assured her there actually was a ghost, she was frightened as never before in her life and begged him not to utter a word about it before he had made another trial of the matter, quite coolly, with her. That night, however, they, as well as the faithful servant who accompanied them, heard the same inexplicable ghostly noise; and only their pressing desire to get rid of the castle at any price enabled them to stifle their terror in the presence of the servant and blame the thing on some petty, accidental cause that would certainly come to light. On the evening of the third day, when the two, with pounding hearts, again climbed the stairs to the guest room, resolved to get to the bottom of the business, they discovered the watchdog, whom somebody had unchained, in front of the door, and, without knowing exactly why, perhaps from an instinctive desire to have the company of some third living creature, they took the dog into the room with them.

Around eleven o'clock, with two candlesticks burning on the table, the couple sat down on separate beds, the Marquise fully clothed, the Marquis with sword and pistols, which he had taken from the closet, at his side; and while they tried as best they could to pass the time in conversation, the dog curled up in the center of the floor and went to sleep. Then, at the stroke of midnight, the dreadful noise was heard again; somebody whom no human eye could see got up on crutches in the corner of the room; there was the sound of straw rustling under him; and at the first step: tap! tap! the dog awakened, started to its feet with its ears pricked up, and backed away to the stove, growling and barking, as if somebody were walking toward it. At this sight the Marquise, her hair standing on end, plunged from the room; and while the Marquis seized his sword and shouted, "Who's there?", slashing the air like a maniac in every direction when there was no answer, she called for her coach, determined to drive to town that instant. But before she had even clattered out of the gate, after snatching up a few belongings, she saw the castle go up in flames all around her. The Marquis, maddened with terror, had caught up a candle and, weary of his life, set fire to every corner of the place, which was paneled in wood throughout. Vainly she sent people in to save the unfortunate man; he had already perished in the most pitiful way, and even today his white bones, which the country people gathered together, rest in the corner of the room from which he had ordered the beggarwoman of Locarno to get up.

*Translated by Martin Greenberg*

GOTTFRIED KELLER

# A Little Legend of the Dance

SAINT GREGORY relates in his tales that Musa was the dancer among the saints. She was the child of good folk, and a graceful little maiden who diligently served the Mother of God and knew only one passion, a love of dancing so uncontrollable that if the girl was not praying, then she was assuredly dancing. And she danced in every conceivable way. Musa danced with her playmates, with the children, with the young men, and even alone. She danced in her little chamber, in the great hall, in the gardens, and over the meadows, and even when she approached the altar she seemed to be dancing a delicious measure rather than walking. And on the smooth marble flags at the church door she never forgot to try a few hasty steps.

Indeed, one day, when she happened to be alone in church, she could not refrain from dancing a few figures in front of the altar and, so to speak, dancing a pretty prayer to the Virgin. She forgot herself so utterly that she fancied she was dreaming when an elderly but handsome gentleman came dancing toward her and supplemented her figures so deftly that between them the two performed the most finished *pas de deux*. The gentleman wore a royal robe of purple and a golden crown on his head, and had a glossy black beard lightly silvered with age as by distant starlight. And music sounded from the choir, for half a dozen cherubs were sitting or standing there on the top of the screen swinging their chubby little legs over it while they played or blew divers instruments. And the urchins made themselves quite comfortable, for each propped his music against one of the stone angels that adorned the choir screen. But the smallest, a round-cheeked piper, was an exception, for he crossed his legs and contrived to hold his music in his rosy toes. And he was the most zealous of all. The others swung their feet, stretched their rustling wings till they shimmered like the breasts of doves, and teased each other as they played.

Musa found no time to wonder at all this until the dance, which lasted some time, was over. The merry gentleman seemed to enjoy it as much as the maiden, who, for her part, might have been tripping about in heaven. But when the music stopped and Musa stood there panting, she began to be really afraid and looked at the old gentleman in amazement, for he was neither out of breath nor hot. He began to speak and introduced himself as David, the royal ancestor of Mary the Virgin, and her messenger. He asked her whether she would like to pass an eternity of bliss in an endless dance of joy, a dance compared with which the one they had just ended could only be called a dismal crawl.

She promptly replied that she could wish for nothing better. Whereupon the blessed King David rejoined that all she had to do was to give up all dancing and all joy for the rest of her earthly days and dedicate herself to penitence and spiritual exercises, and that without faltering or relapse.

At this the maiden was somewhat taken aback, and asked whether she must give up dancing altogether. She doubted whether there really was dancing in heaven, for there was a time for everything. Solid earth seemed a good and suitable place for dancing. Therefore heaven must have other things to offer; otherwise death would simply be superfluous.

David explained to her how sorely she was in error, and proved by many passages from the Bible, as by his own example, that dancing was certainly a blessed occupation for the blessed. But now she must make up her mind quickly, yes or no, whether by temporal renunciation she wished to enter into eternal bliss, or not; if not, he must be getting along, as heaven was in need of a few dancers.

Musa still stood there irresolute, her fingertips playing anxiously about her mouth. It seemed too hard never to dance again just for the sake of an unknown reward.

Then David made a sign and suddenly the musicians played a few bars of a dance, so incredibly blissful and unearthly that the maiden's soul leaped in her body and she twitched in every limb. But she could not move one of them to the measure, and she saw that her body was too stiff and heavy for that music. Full of longing, she thrust her hand into the King's and gave her promise.

Forthwith he vanished and the cherub musicians whirred and fluttered and crowded away through an open window in the church, but first they rolled up their music sheets and, like mischievous children, slapped the patient angels' faces till the church re-echoed.

Musa walked home with devout steps, the heavenly melody in her ears. She had a coarse garment made, laid aside all her fine raiment, and put it on. Then she built a cell in the back of her parents' garden where the shadows of the trees lay thick, made a little bed of moss in it, and lived thenceforth apart from her companions as a penitent and a saint. She passed all her time in prayer, and often scourged herself.

But her severest penance was to keep her limbs still and rigid. As soon as there was a single sound in the air, the twittering of a bird or the rustling of the leaves in the trees, her feet twitched and felt that they must dance. Because this involuntary twitching would not disappear and sometimes, before she was even aware of it, she could not suppress a little pirouette, she had her frail feet bound together with a light chain. Her relatives and friends marveled day and night at the change, but rejoiced in the possession of such a saint and guarded the hermitage under the trees as the apple of their eye. Many came for counsel and intercession. Above all, young maidens were brought to her who were a little heavy on their feet, for it had been noticed that any she touched became light and graceful of movement.

So she passed three years in her solitude, and toward the end of the third year Musa had become almost as thin and transparent as a summer cloud. She no longer moved from her little bed of moss, and lay looking longingly up to heaven. She thought that she could see the golden soles of the blessed dancing and gliding through the blue.

One raw autumn day the news went round that the saint was lying at the point of death. She had had her dark penitential robe taken from her and was clad in dazzling white bridal garments. So she lay with folded hands and smilingly awaited the hour of death.

The whole garden was filled with pious people, the breezes whispered, and the leaves were falling from the trees on every hand. But imperceptibly the whispering of the trees passed into music, which seemed to sound in every treetop, and when the people looked up, lo! everything was clothed in tender green. The myrtles and pomegranates bloomed in fragrance. The earth was decked with flowers, and a rose-colored light lay on the frail form of the dying maiden.

At that moment she gave up the ghost. The chain on her feet sprang asunder with a clear ringing sound. Heaven opened wide, full of infinite splendor, so that all might see beyond. Host upon host of lovely maidens and youths in utmost glory could be seen dancing in endless circles. A splendid King, enthroned on a cloud with a band of six cherubs sitting on its edge, descended a little toward earth and received the form of the blessed Musa before the eyes of all those who filled the garden. They saw how she was borne up to heaven, and forthwith danced out of sight amid the singing of the shining hosts.

In heaven it was high festival. On festal days, however (this is contested by Saint Gregory of Nyssa, but maintained by his namesake of Nazianzus), it was the custom to invite the Muses, who were sitting in hell, into heaven to lend a hand. They were well entertained, but when their work was done, they had to go back to the other place.

When the dances and all the ceremonies were at an end, and the heavenly hosts sat down to table, Musa was led to the table where the nine Muses were sitting. They sat huddled together, half-intimidated, staring round them with their eyes of fiery black or deep blue. Busy Martha from the Gospel served them with her own hands. She had put on her best kitchen apron and had a dainty little smudge on her white chin, and she kindly pressed the good things on the Muses. But it was only when Musa and Saint Cecilia and other women famed in art came along and cheerily greeted the shy Pierians and sat down beside them that they brightened up and grew confidential, while a charming gaiety spread over the whole circle of the women. Musa sat beside Terpsichore, and Cecilia between Polyhymnia and Euterpe, and they all held one another's hands. Then the little cherub musicians came up and made much of the beautiful women, hoping to get some of the shining fruit on the ambrosial table. King David came too in person and brought a golden goblet from which all drank. He passed kindly round the table, not forgetting to pat the lovely Erato's chin as he passed. As things were going so merrily at the Muses' table, our dear Lady herself appeared in all her beauty and goodness, to sit with the Muses awhile. She tenderly kissed the august Urania on the mouth under her starry coronal, and as she said good-by, whispered that she would not rest until the Muses should again sit in paradise forever.

But it did not turn out so. To show their gratitude for the kindness shown them, the Muses took counsel together, and in a distant corner of the underworld, practiced a hymn of praise, to which they tried to give the form of the solemn chorales usual in heaven. They divided into two groups of four voices each, with Urania singing a kind of descant, and so produced a remarkable piece of music.

When the next festival was celebrated in heaven, and the Muses were again on duty, they took advantage of a moment that seemed favorable, grouped themselves, and softly began their song, which soon swelled into a mighty chorus. But in those spaces it sounded so somber—nay, defiant and harsh—so heavy with longing, and so complaining, that at first a terrified silence reigned. Then the whole assembly was seized by earthly suffering and the yearning for earth, and a general weeping broke out.

Endless sighs throbbed through heaven. All the Elders and Prophets started up, terrified and dismayed, while the Muses, with the best intentions, sang ever louder and more sadly. All paradise, with the Patriarchs, the Elders, and the Prophets, all who had ever walked or lain on green pastures, were quite beside themselves. But at last the Holy Trinity itself came up to set things right, and silenced the zealous Muses with a long rolling peal of thunder.

Then peace and serenity returned to heaven, but the poor sisters had to depart; they have never been allowed to return since.

*Translated by M.D. Hottinger*

## ANTON CHEKHOV

# After the Theatre

NADYA ZELENIN and her mother had returned from a performance of *Eugene Onegin* at the theatre. Going into her room, the girl swiftly threw off her dress and let her hair down. Then she quickly sat at the table in her petticoat and white bodice to write a letter like Tatyana's.

"I love you," she wrote, "but you don't love me, you don't love me!"

Having written this, she laughed.

She was only sixteen and had never loved anyone yet. She knew that Gorny (an army officer) and Gruzdyov (a student) were both in love with her, but now, after the opera, she wanted to doubt their love. To be unloved and miserable: what an attractive idea! There was something beautiful, touching and romantic about A loving B when B wasn't interested in A. Onegin was attractive in not loving at all, while Tatyana was enchanting because she loved greatly. Had they loved equally and been happy they might have seemed boring.

"Do stop telling me you love me because I don't believe you," Nadya wrote on, with Gorny, the officer, in mind. "You are highly intelligent, well-educated and serious, you're a brilliant man—with a dazzling future, perhaps—whereas I'm a dull girl, a nobody. As you're perfectly well aware, I should only be a burden to you. Yes, you have taken a fancy to me, I know, you thought you'd found your ideal woman. But that was a mistake. You're already wondering frantically why you ever had to meet such a girl and only your good nature prevents you admitting as much."

Nadya began to feel sorry for herself, and burst into tears.

"I can't bear to leave my mother and brother," she went on, "or else I'd take the veil and go off into the blue, and you'd be free to love another. Oh, if only I were dead!"

Tears blurred what Nadya had written, while rainbow flashes shimmered on table, floor and ceiling, as if she was looking through a prism. Writing was impossible, so she lolled back in her arm-chair and began thinking of Gorny.

How attractive, ye gods, how seductive men were! Nadya remembered what a beautiful expression—pleading, guilty, gentle—Gorny wore whenever anyone discussed music with him and what efforts it cost him to keep a ring of enthusiasm out of his voice. In a society where coolness, hauteur and nonchalance are judged signs of breeding and good manners, one must hide one's passions. Hide them he does, but without success, and it's common knowledge that he's mad about music. Those endless arguments about music, the brash verdicts of ignoramuses . . . they keep him constantly on edge, making him scared, timid, taciturn. He plays the piano magnificently, like a professional pianist, and he might well have been a famous musician had he not been in the army.

Nadya's tears dried and she remembered Gorny declaring his love to her: at a symphony concert and then by the coat-hooks downstairs, with a draught blowing in all directions.

"I'm so glad you've met my student friend Gruzdyov at last," she wrote on. "He is very bright and you're sure to like him. He came to see us yesterday and stayed until two in the morning. We were all delighted and I was sorry you hadn't joined us. He made many remarkable observations."

Putting her hands on the table, Nadya leant her

head on them, and her hair covered the letter. She remembered that Gruzdyov also loved her, that he had as much right to a letter as Gorny. Wouldn't it be better, actually, to write to Gruzdyov? Happiness stirred spontaneously in her breast. First it was small and rolled about like a rubber ball, then it swelled broader and bigger and surged on like a wave. Now Nadya had forgotten Gorny and Gruzdyov, her mind was muddled and ever greater grew her joy. It moved from breast to arms and legs, and she felt as if a light, cool breeze had fanned her head and stirred her hair. Her shoulders shook with silent laughter, the table and lamp-chimney trembled too, and her tears sprinkled the letter. Unable to stop laughing, she quickly thought of something funny to prove that she wasn't laughing about nothing.

"What a funny poodle!" she brought out, feeling as if she was choking with laughter. "How funny that poodle was!"

She had remembered Gruzdyov romping with Maxim, the family poodle, after tea yesterday and then telling a story about a very clever poodle chasing a raven in some yard. The raven had turned round and spoken: "Oh, you wretched little dog." Not knowing that it was involved with a talking raven, the poodle had been terribly embarrassed. It had retreated, baffled, and started barking.

"No, I'd rather love Gruzdyov," Nadya decided, tearing up the letter.

She began thinking of the student, of his love, of her love, but the upshot was that her head swam and she thought about everything at once: mother, street, pencil, piano.

She thought happily and found everything simply wonderful. And this was only the beginning, happiness whispered to her, before long things would be even better still. Soon spring would come, and summer. She and Mother would go to Gorbiki, Gorny would have leave and he would walk round the garden with her, dancing attendance. Gruzdyov would come too. They would play croquet and skittles together, and he would make funny or surprising remarks. Garden, darkness, clear skies, stars . . . she yearned for them passionately. Once more her shoulders shook with laughter and she seemed to smell wormwood in the room, seemed to hear a bough slap the window.

She went and sat on her bed. Not knowing how to cope with the immense happiness which weighed her down, she gazed at the icon hanging at the head of her bed.

"Lord, how marvellous!" she said.

*Translated by Ronald Hingley*

## GIOVANNI VERGA

# The Wolf

SHE WAS TALL AND SLIM, and though no longer young, had the strong firm breasts of the dark-haired woman. She was pale, as if she suffered permanently from malaria, and out of that pallor her cool red lips and her huge eyes devoured you.

In the village they called her "The Wolf" because she could never be sated. The women would cross themselves when they saw her passing, with the cautiously ambling pace of a hungry wolf, alone like an ill-tempered bitch. She could deprive them of their sons and husbands in the twinkling of an eye, with those red lips of hers, and one look from her devilish eyes could make them run after her skirts, from the altar of Saint Agrippina herself. It was a good thing the Wolf never came to church, even at Easter or Christmas, either for mass or for confession. Father Angiolino of the Church of Saint Mary of Jesus, a true servant of the Lord, had lost his soul on her account.

Poor Maricchia, a good and decent girl, cried secretly, because she was the Wolf's daughter and no one would marry her, though she had finery enough in her bottom drawer, and as good a piece of sunny land as any girl in the village.

One day the Wolf fell in love with a good-looking lad just back from the army, who was cutting hay with her in the notary's field. She was so much in love that she felt her flesh burning under the cotton of her vest, and when she looked into his eyes her throat felt as parched as on a June day down in the hottest part of the valley. But the young lad went on mowing quietly, his face turned towards the cut grass. "What's up with you, Mother Pina?" he said to her. In the immense fields where the crackle of flying cicadas was the only sound under that sun that beat down from straight overhead, the Wolf bundled up handful after handful, sheaf after sheaf, without tiring, without straightening up for a moment or putting her lips to the flask, just to be able to keep behind Nanni, who mowed and mowed, and kept asking her, "What do you want, Mother Pina?"

One night she told him. While the men, tired from the long day's work, were drowsing on the threshing ground, and the dogs howled in the vast darkness of the countryside, she said, "I want *you*. You're as lovely as the sun, and as sweet as honey, and I want you!"

"And *I* want that young daughter of yours!" replied Nanni with a smile.

The Wolf put her hands in her hair and, scratching her head silently, walked away; she didn't come to the threshing ground any more. She saw Nanni again in October, when the olives were being pressed; he was working close to her house, and the screeching of the oil-press kept her awake all night.

She said to her daughter, "Take the sack of olives and come with me."

Nanni was busy shovelling the olives under the millstone, shouting "Ohee!" at the mule to keep him moving.

"Do you want my daughter Maricchia?" asked Mother Pina.

"What are you giving with your daughter Maricchia?" replied Nanni.

"She has everything her father left, and on top of that I'll give her my house. I'll be happy if you leave me a corner of the kitchen where I can spread my mattress."

"If that's it, we can settle in at Christmas," said Nanni.

Nanni was all greasy and grimy with oil and half-fermented olives, and Maricchia wouldn't have him on any terms; but her mother seized her by the hair, in front of the fire-place, and said to her through clenched teeth, "If you don't take him I'll kill you!"

The Wolf looked ill, and people were saying the devil turns hermit in old age. No longer was she seen about, or sitting in front of her door peering out of her mad eyes. When she looked into her son-in-law's face those eyes of hers made him laugh, then fumble for the shred of the Virgin Mary's dress* that he carried as an amulet, and cross himself with it. Maricchia stayed at home feeding the children, and her mother went out to the fields, working with the men like a man, weeding, hoeing, feeding the animals, pruning the vineyards, in the north-east winds of January and in the sirocco of August, when the mules drooped their heads and the men slept face downwards under a north-facing wall. During those hours of "midday sun and afternoon's heat when no decent woman's on her feet," Mother Pina was the only living soul to be seen in the countryside, walking over the blazing stones of the bridle-paths, across the scorched stubble of the vast fields which faded into the heat-haze far, far away towards cloud-covered Etna, where the sky lay heavy on the horizon.

"Wake up!" said the Wolf to Nanni, who was asleep in the ditch under the dusty hedge, his head between his arms. "Wake up! I've brought you some wine to freshen your throat."

Nanni opened his eyes wide in astonishment and stared sleepily at her as she stood facing him, pale,

* When the ornate dresses of statues of the Virgin Mary in Sicilian churches are being renewed, shreds from the old dresses are handed to the parishioners and worn as talismans.

her breasts erect and her eyes black as coal, and he involuntarily raised his hands.

"No! No decent woman's on her feet between midday sun and afternoon's heat!" sobbed Nanni, and with his fingers in his hair he pressed his face against the dry grass at the bottom of the ditch. "Go away, go away! Don't come to the threshing ground."

And the Wolf went away, re-fastening her proud tresses, looking straight in front of her feet with her eyes black as coal as she stepped over the hot stubble.

But she came back to the threshing stead, time and again, and Nanni did not object. And if she was late in coming, in those hours between midday sun and afternoon's heat, he would go with sweat on his brow to the top of the deserted white path to await her; and each time afterwards he would bury his hands in his hair and repeat, "Go away, go away! Don't come to the threshing ground again!"

Maricchia wept day and night, and every time she saw her mother coming back pale and silent from the fields, she pierced her with eyes that burned with tears and jealousy, herself like a wolf cub.

"Wicked creature!" she spat. "You wicked mother!"

"Hold your tongue!"

"Thief! Thief!"

"Hold your tongue!"

"I'll go to the police, I will!"

"All right, go!"

And Maricchia did go, carrying her children, dry-eyed and fearless, like a madwoman, because now she loved the husband they had forced on her, greasy and grimy with oil and half-fermented olives.

The police sergeant sent for Nanni; he threatened him with jail and gallows. Nanni sobbed and tore his hair, but he denied nothing and made no excuses.

"It's temptation!" he said. "It's the temptation of hell!"

He threw himself at the sergeant's feet and begged to be sent to prison.

"For mercy's sake, sergeant, take me away from

this hell! Have me hanged or send me to prison, but don't let me see her again, ever again!"

"No," said the Wolf to the sergeant. "When I gave him the house as a dowry, I kept a corner of the kitchen for myself. The house is mine, and I won't leave it!"

Not long afterwards Nanni was kicked in the chest by his mule, and looked near death, but the priest refused to come with the Holy Sacrament unless the Wolf left the house. The Wolf went, and Nanni prepared to go too, as a good Christian should; he confessed and took communion with such clear signs of repentance that all the neighbors, and many curious, came to weep at the sick man's bedside. And it would have been better for Nanni had he died that day, before the devil could come back to tempt him and enter his body and soul, after he recovered.

"Leave me alone," Nanni begged the Wolf. "For mercy's sake, leave me in peace! I have seen death staring me in the face. Poor Maricchia is in despair. Everyone knows now! It will be better for you and for me if I never see you again."

He would willingly have torn out his own eyes to avoid seeing those of the Wolf, those eyes that had made him lose body and soul when they stared into his. He no longer knew how to free himself from her spell. He paid for masses to be said for the souls in purgatory, and asked the priest and the sergeant for help. At Easter he went to confession, and publicly crawled over the forecourt of the church and licked six hand's-breadths of cobblestones in penance. When the Wolf came to tempt him again, he said:

"Listen: don't come back to the threshing ground, because if you come after me again, as sure as God exists, I'll kill you."

"Kill me," replied the Wolf. "It doesn't matter to me: I don't want to live without you."

When he saw her in the distance coming across the field of green corn he stopped hoeing in the vineyard, and went to pull his axe out of the elm tree. The Wolf saw him coming towards her, pale and wild-eyed, with the axe gleaming in the sun, and did not retreat a single step, did not lower her eyes, but continued to walk towards him, with her hands full of red poppies, devouring him with her black eyes.

"Your soul be cursed!" choked Nanni.

*Translated by Alfred Alexander*

STEPHEN CRANE

# An Episode of War

THE LIEUTENANT'S rubber blanket lay on the ground, and upon it he had poured the company's supply of coffee. Corporals and other representatives of the grimy and hot-throated men who lined the breast-work had come for each squad's portion.

The lieutenant was frowning and serious at this task of division. His lips pursed as he drew with his sword various crevices in the heap, until brown squares of coffee, astoundingly equal in size, appeared on the blanket. He was on the verge of a great triumph in mathematics, and the corporals were thronging forward, each to reap a little square, when suddenly the lieutenant cried out and looked quickly at a man near him as if he suspected it was a case of personal assault. The others cried out also when they saw blood upon the lieutenant's sleeve.

He had winced like a man stung, swayed dangerously, and then straightened. The sound of his hoarse breathing was plainly audible. He looked sadly, mystically, over the breast-work at the green face of a wood, where now were many little puffs of white smoke. During this moment the men about him gazed statuelike and silent, astonished and awed by this catastrophe which happened when catastrophes were not expected—when they had leisure to observe it.

As the lieutenant stared at the wood, they too swung their heads, so that for another instant all hands, still silent, contemplated the distant forest as if their minds were fixed upon the mystery of a bullet's journey.

The officer had, of course, been compelled to take his sword into his left hand. He did not hold it by the hilt. He gripped it at the middle of the blade, awkwardly. Turning his eyes from the hostile wood, he looked at the sword as he held it there, and seemed puzzled as to what to do with it, where to put it. In short, this weapon had of a sudden become a strange thing to him. He looked at it in a kind of stupefaction, as if he had been endowed with a trident, a sceptre, or a spade.

Finally he tried to sheathe it. To sheathe a sword held by the left hand, at the middle of the blade, in a scabbard hung at the left hip, is a feat worthy of a sawdust ring. This wounded officer engaged in a desperate struggle with the sword and the wobbling scabbard, and during the time of it he breathed like a wrestler.

But at this instant the men, the spectators, awoke from their stone-like poses and crowded forward sympathetically. The orderly-sergeant took the sword and tenderly placed it in the scabbard. At the time, he leaned nervously backward, and did not allow even his finger to brush the body of the lieutenant. A wound gives strange dignity to him who bears it. Well men shy from his new and terrible majesty. It is as if the wounded man's hand is upon the curtain which hangs before the revelations of all existence—the meaning of ants, potentates, wars, cities, sunshine, snow, a feather dropped from a bird's wing; and the power of it sheds radiance upon a bloody form, and makes the other men understand sometimes that they are little. His comrades look at him with large eyes thoughtfully. Moreover, they fear vaguely that the weight of a finger upon him might send him headlong, precipitate the tragedy, hurl him at once into the dim, gray unknown. And so the orderly-sergeant, while sheathing the sword, leaned nervously backward.

There were others who proffered assistance. One

timidly presented his shoulder and asked the lieutenant if he cared to lean upon it, but the latter waved him away mournfully. He wore the look of one who knows he is the victim of a terrible disease and understands his helplessness. He again stared over the breast-work at the forest, and then, turning, went slowly rearward. He held his right wrist tenderly in his left hand as if the wounded arm was made of very brittle glass.

And the men in silence stared at the wood, then at the departing lieutenant; then at the wood, then at the lieutenant.

As the wounded officer passed from the line of battle, he was enabled to see many things which as a participant in the fight were unknown to him. He saw a general on a black horse gazing over the lines of blue infantry at the green woods which veiled his problems. An aide galloped furiously, dragged his horse suddenly to a halt, saluted, and presented a paper. It was, for a wonder, precisely like a historical painting.

To the rear of the general and his staff a group, composed of a bugler, two or three orderlies, and the bearer of the corps standard, all upon maniacal horses, were working like slaves to hold their ground, preserve their respectful interval, while the shells boomed in the air about them, and caused their chargers to make furious quivering leaps.

A battery, a tumultuous and shining mass, was swirling toward the right. The wild thud of hoofs, the cries of the riders shouting blame and praise, menace and encouragement, and, last, the roar of the wheels, the slant of the glistening guns, brought the lieutenant to an intent pause. The battery swept in curves that stirred the heart; it made halts as dramatic as the crash of a wave on the rocks, and when it fled onward this aggregation of wheels, levers, motors had a beautiful unity, as if it were a missile. The sound of it was a war-chorus that reached into the depths of man's emotion.

The lieutenant, still holding his arm as if it were

of glass, stood watching this battery until all detail of it was lost, save the figures of the riders, which rose and fell and waved lashes over the black mass.

Later, he turned his eyes toward the battle, where the shooting sometimes crackled like bush fires, sometimes sputtered with exasperating irregularity, and sometimes reverberated like the thunder. He saw the smoke rolling upward and saw crowds of men who ran and cheered, or stood and blazed away at the inscrutable distance.

He came upon some stragglers, and they told him how to find the field hospital. They described its exact location. In fact, these men, no longer having part in the battle, knew more of it than others. They told the performance of every corps, every division, the opinion of every general. The lieutenant, carrying his wounded arm rearward, looked upon them with wonder.

At the roadside a brigade was making coffee and buzzing with talk like a girls' boarding school. Several officers came out to him and inquired concerning things of which he knew nothing. One, seeing his arm, began to scold. "Why, man, that's no way to do. You want to fix that thing." He appropriated the lieutenant and the lieutenant's wound. He cut the sleeve and laid bare the arm, every nerve of which softly fluttered under his touch. He bound his handkerchief over the wound, scolding away in the meantime. His tone allowed one to think that he was in the habit of being wounded every day. The lieutenant hung his head, feeling, in this presence, that he did not know how to be correctly wounded.

The low white tents of the hospital were grouped around an old schoolhouse. There was here a singular commotion. In the foreground two ambulances interlocked wheels in the deep mud. The drivers were tossing the blame of it back and forth, gesticulating and berating, while from the ambulances, both crammed with wounded, there came an occasional groan. An interminable crowd of bandaged men were coming and going. Great numbers sat under the trees nursing heads or arms or legs. There was a dispute of some kind raging on the steps of the schoolhouse. Sitting with his back against a tree a man with a face as gray as a new army blanket was serenely smoking a corncob pipe. The lieutenant wished to rush forward and inform him that he was dying.

A busy surgeon was passing near the lieutenant. "Good morning," he said, with a friendly smile. Then he caught sight of the lieutenant's arm, and his face at once changed. "Well, let's have a look at it." He seemed possessed suddenly of a great contempt for the lieutenant. This wound evidently placed the latter on a very low social plane. The doctor cried out impatiently: "What mutton-head tied it up that way anyhow?" The lieutenant answered, "Oh, a man."

When the wound was disclosed the doctor fingered it disdainfully. "Humph," he said, "You come along with me and I'll tend to you." His voice contained the same scorn as if he were saying, "You will have to go to jail."

The lieutenant had been very meek, but now his face flushed, and he looked into the doctor's eyes. "I guess I won't have it amputated," he said.

"Nonsense, man! Nonsense! Nonsense!" cried the doctor. "Come along, now. I won't amputate it. Come along. Don't be a baby."

"Let go of me," said the lieutenant, holding back wrathfully, his glance fixed upon the door of the old schoolhouse, as sinister to him as the portals of death.

And this is the story of how the lieutenant lost his arm. When he reached home, his sisters, his mother, his wife, sobbed for a long time at the sight of the flat sleeve. "Oh, well," he said, standing shamefaced amid these tears, "I don't suppose it matters so much as all that."

## GUY DE MAUPASSANT

# An Old Man

ALL THE NEWSPAPERS had carried this advertisement:

The new spa at Rondelis offers all the advantages desirable for a lengthy stay or even for permanent residence. Its ferruginous waters, recognized as the best in the world for countering all impurities of the blood, also seem to possess special qualities calculated to prolong human life. This remarkable circumstance may be due in part to the exceptional situation of the little town, which lies in a mountainous region, in the middle of a forest of firs. The fact remains that for several centuries it has been noted for cases of extraordinary longevity.

And the public came along in droves.

One morning the doctor in charge of the springs was asked to call on a newcomer, Monsieur Daron, who had arrived a few days before and had rented a charming villa on the edge of the forest. He was a little old man of eighty-six, still quite sprightly, wiry, healthy and active, who went to infinite pains to conceal his age.

He offered the doctor a seat and started questioning him straight away.

"Doctor," he said, "if I am in good health, it is thanks to careful living. Though not very old, I have already attained a respectable age, yet I keep free of all illnesses and indispositions, even the slightest malaises, by means of careful living. It is said that the climate here is very good for the health. I am perfectly prepared to believe it, but before settling down here I want proof. I am therefore going to ask you to come and see me once a week to give me the following information in detail.

"First of all I wish to have a complete, absolutely complete, list of all the inhabitants of the town and the surrounding area who are over eighty years old. I also need a few physical and physiological details regarding each of them. I wish to know their professions, their way of life, their habits. Every time one of those people dies you will be good enough to inform me, giving me the precise cause of death and describing the circumstances."

Then he added graciously, "I hope, Doctor, that we shall become good friends," and held out his wrinkled little hand. The doctor shook it, promising him his devoted co-operation.

Monsieur Daron had always had an obsessive fear of death. He had deprived himself of nearly all the pleasures of this world because they were dangerous, and whenever anyone expressed surprise that he should not drink wine—wine, that purveyor of dreams and gaiety—he would reply in a voice in which a note of fear could be detected: "I value my life." And he stressed the word *my*, as if that life, *his* life, possessed some special distinction. He put into that *my* such a difference between his life and other people's lives that any rejoinder was out of the question.

For that matter he had a very special way of stressing the possessive pronouns designating parts of his person and even things which belonged to him. When he said "my eyes, my legs, my arms, my hands," it was quite obvious that there must be no mistake about this: those organs were not at all like other people's. But where this distinction was particularly noticeable was in his references to his doctor. When he said "my doctor," one would have thought that that doctor belonged to him and nobody else, destined for him alone, to attend to his illnesses and to nothing else, and that he was superior to all the other doctors in the world, without exception.

He had never regarded other men as anything but puppets of a sort, created to fill up an empty world. He divided them into two classes: those he greeted because some chance had put him in contact with them, and those he did not greet. But both these categories of individuals were equally insignificant in his eyes.

However, beginning with the day when the Rondelis doctor brought him the list of the seventeen inhabitants of the town who were over eighty, he felt a new interest awaken in his heart, an unfamiliar solicitude for these old people whom he was going to see fall by the wayside one by one. He had no desire to make their acquaintance, but he formed a very clear idea of their persons, and when the doctor dined with him, every Thursday, he spoke only of them. "Well, doctor," he would say, "and how is Joseph Poinçot today? We left him feeling a little ill last week." And when the doctor had given him the patient's bill of health, Monsieur Daron would suggest changes in his diet, experiments, methods of treatment which he might later apply to himself if they had succeeded with the others. Those seventeen old people provided him with an experimental field from which he learnt many a lesson.

One evening the doctor announced as he came in: "Rosalie Tournel has died."

Monsieur Daron gave a start and immediately asked, "What of?"

"Of a chill."

The little old man gave a sigh of relief. Then he said, "She was too fat, too heavy; she must have eaten too much. When I get to her age I'll be more careful about my weight." (He was two years older than Rosalie Tournel, but he claimed to be only seventy.)

A few months later it was the turn of Henri Brissot. Monsieur Daron was very upset. This time it was a man, and a thin man at that, within three months of his own age, and careful about his health. He did not dare to ask any questions, but waited anxiously for the doctor to give him some details.

"Oh, so he died just like that, all of a sudden," he said. "But he was perfectly all right last week. He must have done something silly, I suppose, Doctor?"

The doctor, who was enjoying himself, replied: "I don't think so. His children told me he had been very careful."

Then, unable to contain himself any longer, and filled with fear, Monsieur Daron asked: "But . . . but . . . what did he die of, then?"

"Of pleurisy."

The little old man clapped his dry hands in sheer joy.

"I told you so! I told you he had done something silly. You don't get pleurisy for nothing. He must have gone out for a breath of air after his dinner and the cold must have gone to his chest. Pleurisy! Why, that's an accident, not an illness. Only fools die of pleurisy."

And he ate his dinner in high spirits, talking about those who were left.

"There are only fifteen of them now, but they are all hale and hearty, aren't they? The whole of life is like that: the weakest go first; people who live beyond thirty have a good chance of reaching sixty; those who pass sixty often get to eighty; and those who pass eighty nearly always live to be a hundred, because they are the fittest, toughest and most sensible of all."

Another two disappeared during the year, one of dysentery and the other of a choking fit. Monsieur Daron was highly amused by the death of the former and concluded that he must have eaten something stimulating the day before.

"Dysentery is the disease of careless people. Dammit all, Doctor, you ought to have watched over his diet."

As for the man who had been carried off by a choking fit, his death could only be due to a heart condition which had hitherto gone unnoticed.

But one evening the doctor announced the decease of Paul Timonet, a sort of mummy of whom it had been hoped to make a centenarian and an advertisement for the spa.

When Monsieur Daron asked, as usual: "What did he die of?" the doctor replied, "Bless me, I really don't know."

"What do you mean, you don't know. A doctor always knows. Hadn't he some organic lesion?"

The doctor shook his head.

"No, none."

"Possibly some infection of the liver or the kidneys?"

"No, they were quite sound."

"Did you check whether the stomach was functioning properly? A stroke is often caused by poor digestion."

"There was no stroke."

Monsieur Daron, very perplexed, said excitedly: "Look, he must have died of something! What do you think it was?"

The doctor threw up his hands.

"I've no idea, no idea at all. He died because he died, that's all."

Then Monsieur Daron, in a voice full of emotion, asked: "Exactly how old was that one? I can't remember."

"Eighty-nine."

And the little old man, at once incredulous and reassured, exclaimed:

"Eighty-nine! So whatever it was, it wasn't old age. . . ."

*Translated by Roger Colet*

## JOÃO GUIMARÃES ROSA

# The Third Bank of the River

MY FATHER was a dutiful, orderly, straightforward man. And according to several reliable people of whom I inquired, he had had these qualities since adolescence or even childhood. By my own recollection, he was neither jollier nor more melancholy than the other men we knew. Maybe a little quieter. It was Mother, not Father, who ruled the house. She scolded us daily—my sister, my brother, and me. But it happened one day that Father ordered a boat.

He was very serious about it. It was to be made specially for him, of mimosa wood. It was to be sturdy enough to last twenty or thirty years and just large enough for one person. Mother carried on plenty about it. Was her husband going to become a fisherman all of a sudden? Or a hunter? Father said nothing. Our house was less than a mile from the river, which around there was deep, quiet, and so wide you couldn't see across it.

I can never forget the day the rowboat was delivered. Father showed no joy or other emotion. He just put on his hat as he always did and said good-by to us. He took along no food or bundle of any sort. We expected Mother to rant and rave, but she didn't. She looked very pale and bit her lip, but all she said was: "If you go away, stay away. Don't ever come back!"

Father made no reply. He looked gently at me and motioned me to walk along with him. I feared

Mother's wrath, yet I eagerly obeyed. We headed toward the river together. I felt bold and exhilarated, so much so that I said: "Father, will you take me with you in your boat?"

He just looked at me, gave me his blessing, and by a gesture, told me to go back. I made as if to do so but, when his back was turned, I ducked behind some bushes to watch him. Father got into the boat and rowed away. Its shadow slid across the water like a crocodile, long and quiet.

Father did not come back. Nor did he go anywhere, really. He just rowed and floated across and around, out there in the river. Everyone was appalled. What had never happened, what could not possibly happen, was happening. Our relatives, neighbors, and friends came over to discuss the phenomenon.

Mother was ashamed. She said little and conducted herself with great composure. As a consequence, almost everyone thought (though no one said it) that Father had gone insane. A few, however, suggested that Father might be fulfilling a promise he had made to God or to a saint, or that he might have some horrible disease, maybe leprosy, and that he left for the sake of the family, at the same time wishing to remain fairly near them.

Travelers along the river and people living near the bank on one side or the other reported that Father never put foot on land, by day or night. He just moved about on the river, solitary, aimless, like a derelict. Mother and our relatives agreed that the food which he had doubtless hidden in the boat would soon give out and that then he would either leave the river and travel off somewhere (which would be at least a little more respectable) or he would repent and come home.

How far from the truth they were! Father had a secret source of provisions: me. Every day I stole food and brought it to him. The first night after he left, we all lit fires on the shore and prayed and called to him. I was deeply distressed and felt a need to do something more. The following day I went down to the river with a loaf of corn bread, a bunch of bananas, and some bricks of raw brown sugar. I waited impatiently a long, long hour. Then I saw the boat, far off, alone, gliding almost imperceptibly on the smoothness of the river. Father was sitting in the bottom of the boat. He saw me but he did not row toward me or make any gesture. I showed him the food and then I placed it in a hollow rock on the river bank; it was safe there from animals, rain, and dew. I did this day after day, on and on and on. Later I learned, to my surprise, that Mother knew what I was doing and left food around where I could easily steal it. She had a lot of feelings she didn't show.

Mother sent for her brother to come and help on the farm and in business matters. She had the schoolteacher come and tutor us children at home because of the time we had lost. One day, at her request, the priest put on his vestments, went down to the shore, and tried to exorcise the devils that had got into my father. He shouted that Father had a duty to cease his unholy obstinacy. Another day she arranged to have two soldiers come and try to frighten him. All to no avail. My father went by in the distance, sometimes so far away he could barely be seen. He never replied to anyone and no one ever got close to him. When some newspapermen came in a launch to take his picture, Father headed his boat to the other side of the river and into the marshes, which he knew like the palm of his hand but in which other people quickly got lost. There in his private maze, which extended for miles, with heavy foliage overhead and rushes on all sides, he was safe.

We had to get accustomed to the idea of Father's being out on the river. We had to but we couldn't, we never could. I think I was the only one who understood to some degree what our father wanted and what he did not want. The thing I could not understand at all was how he stood the hardship. Day and night, in sun and rain, in heat and in the terrible midyear cold spells, with his old hat on his head and very little other clothing, week after week, month after month, year after year, unheedful of the waste and emptiness in which his life was slipping by. He never set foot on earth or grass, on isle or mainland shore. No doubt he sometimes tied up the boat at a secret place, perhaps at the tip of some island, to get a little sleep. He never lit a fire or even struck a match and he had no flashlight. He took only a small part of the food that I left in the hollow rock—not enough, it seemed to me, for survival. What could his state of health have been? How about the continual drain on his energy, pulling and pushing the oars to control the boat? And how did he survive the annual floods, when the river rose and swept along with it all sorts of dangerous objects—branches of trees, dead bodies of animals—that might suddenly crash against his little boat?

He never talked to a living soul. And we never talked about him. We just thought. No, we could never put our father out of mind. If for a short time we seemed to, it was just a lull from which we would be sharply awakened by the realization of his frightening situation.

My sister got married, but Mother didn't want a wedding party. It would have been a sad affair, for we thought of him every time we ate some especially tasty food. Just as we thought of him in our cozy beds on a cold, stormy night—out there, alone and unprotected, trying to bail out the boat with only his hands and a gourd. Now and then someone would say that I was getting to look more and more like my father. But I knew that by then his hair and beard must have been shaggy and his nails long. I pictured him thin and sickly, black with hair and sunburn, and almost naked despite the articles of clothing I occasionally left for him.

He didn't seem to care about us at all. But I felt affection and respect for him, and, whenever they praised me because I had done something good, I said: "My father taught me to act that way."

It wasn't exactly accurate but it was a truthful sort of lie. As I said, Father didn't seem to care about us. But then why did he stay around there? Why didn't he go up the river or down the river, beyond the possibility of seeing us or being seen by us? He alone knew the answer.

My sister had a baby boy. She insisted on showing Father his grandson. One beautiful day we all went down to the riverbank, my sister in her white wedding dress, and she lifted the baby high. Her husband held a parasol above them. We shouted to Father and waited. He did not appear. My sister cried; we all cried in each other's arms.

My sister and her husband moved far away. My brother went to live in a city. Times changed, with their usual imperceptible rapidity. Mother finally moved too; she was old and went to live with her daughter. I remained behind, a leftover. I could never think of marrying. I just stayed there with the impedimenta of my life. Father, wandering alone and forlorn on the river, needed me. I knew he needed me, although he never even told me why he was doing it. When I put the question to people bluntly and insistently, all they told me was that they heard that Father had explained it to the man who made the boat. But now this man was dead and nobody knew or remembered anything. There was just some foolish talk, when the rains were especially severe and persistent, that my father was wise like Noah and had the boat built in anticipation of a new flood; I dimly remember people saying this. In any case, I would not condemn my father for what he was doing. My hair was beginning to turn gray.

I have only sad things to say. What bad had I done, what was my great guilt? My father always away and his absence always with me. And the river, always the river, perpetually renewing itself. The river, always. I was beginning to suffer from old age, in which life is just a sort of lingering. I had attacks of illness and of anxiety. I had a nagging rheumatism. And he? Why, why was he doing it? He must have been suffering terribly. He was so old. One day, in his failing strength, he might let the boat capsize; or he might let the current carry it downstream, on and on, until it plunged over the waterfall to the boiling turmoil below. It pressed upon my heart. He was out there and I was forever robbed of my peace. I am guilty of I know not what, and my pain is an open wound inside me. Perhaps I would know—if things were different. I began to guess what was wrong.

Out with it! Had I gone crazy? No, in our house that word was never spoken, never through all the years. No one called anybody crazy, for nobody is crazy. Or maybe everybody. All I did was go there and wave a handkerchief so he would be more likely to see me. I was in complete command of myself. I waited. Finally he appeared in the distance, there, then over there, a vague shape sitting in the back of the boat. I called to him several times. And I said what I was so eager to say, to state formally and under oath. I said it as loud as I could:

"Father, you have been out there long enough. You are old. . . . Come back, you don't have to do it anymore. . . . Come back and I'll go instead. Right now, if you want. Any time. I'll get into the boat. I'll take your place."

And when I had said this my heart beat more firmly.

He heard me. He stood up. He maneuvered with his oars and headed the boat toward me. He had accepted my offer. And suddenly I trembled, down deep. For he had raised his arm and waved—the first time in so many, so many years. And I couldn't. . . . In terror, my hair on end, I ran, I fled madly. For he seemed to come from another world. And I'm begging forgiveness, begging, begging.

I experienced the dreadful sense of cold that comes from deadly fear, and I became ill. Nobody ever saw or heard about him again. Am I a man, after such a failure? I am what never should have been. I am what must be silent. I know it is too late. I must stay in the deserts and unmarked plains of my life, and I fear I shall shorten it. But when death comes I want them to take me and put me in a little boat in this perpetual water between the long shores; and I, down the river, lost in the river, inside the river . . . the river. . . .

*Translated by William L. Grossman*

## SHOLOM ALEICHEM

# A Yom Kippur Scandal

"THAT'S NOTHING!" called out the man with round eyes, like an ox, who had been sitting all this time in a corner by the window, smoking and listening to our stories of thefts, robberies, and expropriations. "I'll tell you a story of a theft that took place in our town, in the synagogue itself, and on Yom Kippur at that! It is worth listening to.

"Our town, Kasrilevke—that's where I'm from, you know—is a small town, and a poor one. There is no thievery there. No one steals anything for the simple reason that there is nobody to steal from and nothing worth stealing. And besides, a Jew is not a thief by nature. That is, he may be a thief, but not the sort who will climb through a window or attack you with a knife. He will divert, pervert, subvert, and contravert as a matter of course; but he won't pull anything out of your pocket. He won't be caught like a common thief and led through the streets with a yellow placard on his back. Imagine, then, a theft taking place in Kasrilevke, and such a theft at that. Eighteen hundred rubles at one crack.

"Here is how it happened. One Yom Kippur eve, just before the evening services, a stranger arrived in our town, a salesman of some sort from Lithuania. He left his bag at an inn and went forth immediately to look for a place of worship, and he came upon the old synagogue. Coming in just before the service began, he found the trustees around the collection plates. '*Sholem aleichem,*' said he.

'*Aleichem sholem,*' they answered. 'Where does our guest hail from?' 'From Lithuania.' 'And your name?' 'Even your grandmother wouldn't know if I told her.' 'But you have come to our synagogue!' 'Where else should I go?' 'Then you want to pray here?' 'Can I help myself? What else can I do?' 'Then put something into the plate.' 'What did you think? That I was not going to pay?'

"To make a long story short, our guest took out three silver rubles and put them in the plate. Then he put a ruble into the cantor's plate, one into the rabbi's, gave one for the *cheder,* threw a half into the charity box, and then began to divide money among the poor who flocked to the door. And in our town we have so many poor people that if you really wanted to start giving, you could divide Rothschild's fortune among them.

"Impressed by his generosity, the men quickly found a place for him along the east wall. Where did they find room for him when all the places along the wall are occupied? Don't ask. Have you ever been at a celebration—a wedding or circumcision—when all the guests are already seated at the table, and suddenly there is a commotion outside—the rich uncle has arrived? What do you do? You push and shove and squeeze until a place is made for the rich relative. Squeezing is a Jewish custom. If no one squeezes us, we squeeze each other."

The man with the eyes that bulged like an ox's paused, looked at the crowd to see what effect his wit had on us, and went on.

"So our guest went up to his place of honor and called to the *shammes* to bring him a praying stand. He put on his *tallis* and started to pray. He prayed and he prayed, standing on his feet all the time. He never sat down or left his place all evening long or all the next day. To fast all day standing on one's feet, without ever sitting down—that only a Litvak can do!

"But when it was all over, when the final blast of

the *shofar* had died down, the Day of Atonement had ended, and Chaim the *melamed,* who had led the evening prayers after Yom Kippur from time immemorial, had cleared his throat, and in his tremulous voice had already begun—'*Ma-a riv a-ro-vim* . . .' suddenly screams were heard. 'Help! Help! Help!' We looked around: the stranger was stretched out on the floor in a dead faint. We poured water on him, revived him, but he fainted again. What was the trouble? Plenty! This Litvak tells us that he had brought with him to Kasrilevke eighteen hundred rubles. To leave that much at the inn—think of it, eighteen hundred rubles—he had been afraid. Whom could he trust with such a sum of money in a strange town? And yet, to keep it in his pocket on Yom Kippur was not exactly proper either. So at last this plan had occurred to him: he had taken the money to the synagogue and slipped it into the praying stand. Only a Litvak could do a thing like that! . . . Now do you see why he had not stepped away from the praying stand for a single minute? And yet during one of the many prayers when we all turn our face to the wall, someone must have stolen the money. . . .

"Well, the poor man wept, tore his hair, wrung his hands. What would he do with the money gone? It was not his own money, he said. He was only a clerk. The money was his employer's. He himself was a poor man, with a houseful of children. There was nothing for him to do now but go out and drown himself, or hang himself right here in front of everybody.

"Hearing these words, the crowd stood petrified, forgetting that they had all been fasting since the night before and it was time to go home and eat. It was a disgrace before a stranger, a shame and a scandal in our own eyes. A theft like that—eighteen hundred rubles! And where? In the Holy of Holies, in the old synagogue of Kasrilevke. And on what day? On the holiest day of the year, on Yom Kippur! Such a thing had never been heard of before.

" '*Shammes*, lock the door!' ordered our rabbi. We have our own rabbi in Kasrilevke, Reb Yozifel, a true man of God, a holy man. Not too sharpwitted, perhaps, but a good man, a man with no bitterness in him. Sometimes he gets ideas that you would not hit upon if you had eighteen heads on your shoulders. . . . When the door was locked, Reb Yozifel turned to the congregation, his face pale as death and his hands trembling, his eyes burning with a strange fire.

"He said, 'Listen to me, my friends. This is an ugly thing, a thing unheard of since the world was created—that here in Kasrilevke there should be a sinner, a renegade to his people, who would have the audacity to take from a stranger, a poor man with a family, a fortune like this. And on what day? On the holiest day of the year, on Yom Kippur, and perhaps at the last, most solemn moment—just before the *shofar* was blown! Such a thing has never happened anywhere. I cannot believe it is possible. It simply cannot be. But perhaps—who knows? Man is greedy, and the temptation—especially with a sum like this, eighteen hundred rubles, God forbid—is great enough. So if one of us was tempted, if he were fated to commit this evil on a day like this, we must probe the matter thoroughly, strike at the root of this whole affair. Heaven and earth have sworn that the truth must always rise as oil upon the waters. Therefore, my friends, let us search each other now, go through each other's garments, shake out our pockets—all of us from the oldest householder to the *shammes*, not leaving anyone out. Start with me. Search my pockets first.'

"Thus spoke Reb Yozifel, and he was the first to unbind his gabardine and turn his pockets inside out. And following his example all the men loosened their girdles and showed the linings of their pockets, too. They searched each other, they felt and shook one another, until they came to Lazer Yossel, who turned all colors and began to argue that, in the first place, the stranger was a swindler, that his story was the pure fabrication of a Litvak. No one had stolen any money from him. Couldn't they see that it was all a falsehood and a lie?

"The congregation began to clamor and shout. What did he mean by this? All the important men had allowed themselves to be searched, so why should Lazer Yossel escape? There are no privileged characters here. 'Search him! Search him!' the crowd roared.

"Lazer Yossel saw that it was hopeless, and began to plead for mercy with tears in his eyes. He begged them not to search him. He swore by all that was holy that he was as innocent in this as he would want to be of any wrongdoing as long as he lived. Then why didn't he want to be searched? It was a disgrace to him, he said. He begged them to have pity on his youth, not to bring this disgrace down on him. 'Do anything you wish with me,' he said, 'but don't touch my pockets.' How do you like that? Do you suppose we listened to him?

"But wait . . . I forgot to tell you who this Lazer Yossel was. He was not a Kasrilevkite himself. He came from the devil knows where, at the time of his marriage, to live with his wife's parents. The rich man of our town had dug him up somewhere for his daughter, boasted that he had found a rare nugget, a fitting match for a daughter like his. He knew a thousand pages of *Talmud* by heart, and all of the Bible. He was a master of Hebrew, arithmetic, bookkeeping, algebra, penmanship—in short, everything you could think of. When he arrived in Kasrilevke—this jewel of a young man—everyone came out to gaze at him. What sort of bargain had the rich man picked out? Well, to look at him you could tell nothing. He was a young man, something in trousers. Not bad looking, but with a nose a trifle too long, eyes that burned like two coals, and a sharp tongue. Our leading citizens began to work on him: tried him out on a page of *Gemara,* a chapter from the Scriptures, a bit of Rambam, this, that, and the other. He was perfect in everything, the dog! Whenever you went after him, he was at home. Reb Yozifel himself said that he could have been a rabbi in any Jewish congregation. As for world affairs, there is nothing to talk about. We have an authority on such things in our town, Zaidel Reb Shaye's, but he could not hold a candle to Lazer Yossel. And when it came to chess—there was no one like him in all the world! Talk about versatile people. . . . Naturally the whole town envied the rich man his find, but some of them felt he was a little too good to be true. He was too clever (and too much of anything is bad!). For a man of his station he was too free and easy, a hail-fellow-well-met, too familiar with all the young folk—boys, girls, and maybe even loose women. There were rumors. . . . At the same time he went around alone too much, deep in thought. At the synagogue he came in last, put on his *tallis,* and with his skullcap on askew, thumbed aimlessly through his prayerbook without ever following the services. No one ever saw him doing anything exactly wrong, and yet people murmured that he was not a God-fearing man. Apparently a man cannot be perfect. . . .

"And so, when his turn came to be searched and he refused to let them do it, that was all the proof most of the men needed that he was the one who had taken the money. He begged them to let him swear any oath they wished, begged them to chop him, roast him, cut him up—do anything but shake his pockets out. At this point even our rabbi, Reb Yozifel, although he was a man we had never seen angry, lost his temper and started to shout.

" 'You!' he cried. 'You thus and thus! Do you know what you deserve? You see what all these men have endured. They were able to forget the disgrace and allowed themselves to be searched; but you want to be the only exception! God in heaven! Either confess and hand over the money, or let us see for ourselves what is in your pockets. You are trifling now with the entire Jewish community. Do you know what they can do to you?'

"To make a long story short, the men took hold of this young upstart, threw him down on the floor with force, and began to search him all over, shake out every one of his pockets. And finally they shook out. . . . Well, guess what! A couple of well-gnawed chicken bones and a few dozen plum pits still moist from chewing. You can imagine what an impression this made—to discover food in the pockets of our prodigy on this holiest of fast days. Can you imagine the look on the young man's face, and on his father-in-law's? And on that of our poor rabbi?

"Poor Reb Yozifel! He turned away in shame. He could look no one in the face. On Yom Kippur, and in his synagogue. . . . As for the rest of us, hungry as we were, we could not stop talking about it all the way home. We rolled with laughter in the streets. Only Reb Yozifel walked home alone, his head bowed, full of grief, unable to look anyone in the eyes, as though the bones had been shaken out of his own pockets."

The story was apparently over. Unconcerned, the man with the round eyes of an ox turned back to the window and resumed smoking.

"Well," we all asked in one voice, "and what about the money?"

"What money?" asked the man innocently, watching the smoke he had exhaled.

"What do you mean—what money? The eighteen hundred rubles!"

"Oh," he drawled. "The eighteen hundred. They were gone."

"Gone?"

"Gone forever."

*Translated by Julius and Frances Butwin*

## I. L. PERETZ

# If Not Higher

EARLY EVERY FRIDAY MORNING, at the time of the Penitential Prayers, the rabbi of Nemirov would vanish.

He was nowhere to be seen—neither in the synagogue nor in the two Houses of Study nor at a *minyan.* And he was certainly not at home. His door stood open; whoever wished could go in and out; no one would steal from the rabbi. But not a living creature was within.

Where could the rabbi be? Where should he be? In heaven, no doubt. A rabbi has plenty of business to take care of just before the Days of Awe. Jews, God bless them, need livelihood, peace, health, and good matches. They want to be pious and good, but our sins are so great, and Satan of the thousand eyes watches the whole earth from one end to the other. What he sees he reports; he denounces, informs. Who can help us if not the rabbi!

That's what the people thought.

But once a Litvak came, and he laughed. You know the Litvaks. They think little of the Holy Books but stuff themselves with Talmud and law. So this Litvak points to a passage in the Gemara—it sticks in your eyes—where it is written that even Moses our Teacher did not ascend to heaven during his lifetime but remained suspended two and a half feet below. Go argue with a Litvak!

So where can the rabbi be?

"That's not my business," said the Litvak, shrugging. Yet all the while—what a Litvak can do!—he is scheming to find out.

That same night, right after the evening prayers, the Litvak steals into the rabbi's room, slides under the rabbi's bed, and waits. He'll watch all night and discover where the rabbi vanishes and what he does during the Penitential Prayers.

Someone else might have got drowsy and fallen asleep, but a Litvak is never at a loss; he recites a whole tractate of the Talmud by heart.

At dawn he hears the call to prayers.

The rabbi has already been awake for a long time. The Litvak has heard him groaning for a whole hour.

Whoever has heard the rabbi of Nemirov groan knows how much sorrow for all Israel, how much suffering, lies in each groan. A man's heart might break, hearing it. But a Litvak is made of iron; he listens and remains where he is. The rabbi—long life to him!—lies on the bed, and the Litvak under the bed.

Then the Litvak hears the beds in the house begin to creak; he hears people jumping out of their beds, mumbling a few Jewish words, pouring water on their fingernails, banging doors. Everyone has left. It is again quiet and dark; a bit of light from the moon shines through the shutters.

(Afterward the Litvak admitted that when he found himself alone with the rabbi a great fear took hold of him. Goose pimples spread across his skin, and the roots of his earlocks pricked him like needles. A trifle: to be alone with the rabbi at the time of the Penitential Prayers! But a Litvak is stubborn. So he quivered like a fish in water and remained where he was.)

Finally the rabbi—long life to him!—arises. First he does what befits a Jew. Then he goes to the clothes closet and takes out a bundle of peasant clothes: linen trousers, high boots, a coat, a big felt hat, and a long wide leather belt studded with brass nails. The rabbi gets dressed. From his coat pocket dangles the end of a heavy peasant rope.

The rabbi goes out, and the Litvak follows him.

On the way the rabbi stops in the kitchen, bends down, takes an ax from under the bed, puts it in his belt, and leaves the house. The Litvak trembles but continues to follow.

The hushed dread of the Days of Awe hangs over the dark streets. Every once in a while a cry rises from some *minyan* reciting the Penitential Prayers, or from a sickbed. The rabbi hugs the sides of the streets, keeping to the shade of the houses. He glides from house to house, and the Litvak after him. The Litvak hears the sound of his heartbeats mingling with the sound of the rabbi's heavy steps. But he keeps on going and follows the rabbi to the outskirts of the town.

A small wood stands behind the town.

The rabbi—long life to him!—enters the wood. He takes thirty or forty steps and stops by a small tree. The Litvak, overcome with amazement, watches the rabbi take the ax out of his belt and strike the tree. He hears the tree creak and fall. The rabbi chops the tree into logs and the logs into sticks. Then he makes a bundle of the wood and ties it with the rope in his pocket. He puts the bundle of wood on his back, shoves the ax back into his belt, and returns to the town.

He stops at a back street beside a small broken-down shack and knocks at the window.

"Who is there?" asks a frightened voice. The Litvak recognizes it as the voice of a sick Jewish woman.

"I," answers the rabbi in the accent of a peasant.

"Who is I?"

Again the rabbi answers in Russian. "Vassil."

"Who is Vassil, and what do you want?"

"I have wood to sell, very cheap." And, not waiting for the woman's reply, he goes into the house.

The Litvak steals in after him. In the gray light of early morning he sees a poor room with broken, miserable furnishings. A sick woman, wrapped in rags, lies on the bed. She complains bitterly, "Buy? How can I buy? Where will a poor widow get money?"

"I'll lend it to you," answers the supposed Vassil. "It's only six cents."

"And how will I ever pay you back?" asks the poor woman, groaning.

"Foolish one," says the rabbi reproachfully. "See, you are a poor sick Jew, and I am ready to trust you with a little wood. I am sure you'll pay. While you, you have such a great and mighty God and you don't trust him for six cents."

"And who will kindle the fire?" asks the widow. "Have I the strength to get up? My son is at work."

"I'll kindle the fire," answers the rabbi.

As the rabbi put the wood into the oven he recited, in a groan, the first portion of the Penitential Prayers.

As he kindled the fire and the wood burned brightly, he recited, a bit more joyously, the second portion of the Penitential Prayers. When the fire was set he recited the third portion, and then he shut the stove.

The Litvak who saw all this became a disciple of the rabbi.

And ever after, when another disciple tells how the rabbi of Nemirov ascends to heaven at the time of the Penitential Prayers, the Litvak does not laugh. He only adds quietly, "If not higher."

*Translated by Marie Syrkin*

# Part Two

JAMES JOYCE

# Eveline

SHE SAT AT THE WINDOW watching the evening invade the avenue. Her head was leaned against the window curtains and in her nostrils was the odor of dusty cretonne. She was tired.

Few people passed. The man out of the last house passed on his way home; she heard his footsteps clacking along the concrete pavement and afterwards crunching on the cinder path before the new red houses. One time there used to be a field there in which they used to play every evening with other people's children. Then a man from Belfast bought the field and built houses in it—not like their little brown houses but bright brick houses with shining roofs. The children of the avenue used to play together in that field—the Devines, the Waters, the Dunns, little Keogh the cripple, she and her brothers and sisters. Ernest, however, never played: he was too grown up. Her father used often to hunt them in out of the field with his blackthorn stick; but usually little Keogh used to keep *nix* and call out when he saw her father coming. Still they seemed to have been rather happy then. Her father was not so bad then; and besides, her mother was alive. That was a long time ago; she and her brothers and sisters were all grown up; her mother was dead. Tizzie Dunn was dead, too, and the Waters had gone back to England. Everything changes. Now she was going to go away like the others, to leave her home.

Home! She looked round the room, reviewing all its familiar objects which she had dusted once a week for so many years, wondering where on earth all the dust came from. Perhaps she would never see again those familiar objects from which she had never dreamed of being divided. And yet during all those years she had never found out the name of the priest whose yellowing photograph hung on the wall above the broken harmonium beside the colored print of the promises made to Blessed Margaret Mary Alacoque. He had been a school friend of her father. Whenever he showed the photograph to a visitor her father used to pass it with a casual word:

—He is in Melbourne now.

She had consented to go away, to leave her home. Was that wise? She tried to weigh each side of the question. In her home anyway she had shelter and food; she had those whom she had known all her life about her. Of course she had to work hard both in the house and at business. What would they say of her in the Stores when they found out that she had run away with a fellow? Say she was a fool, perhaps; and her place would be filled up by advertisement. Miss Gavan would be glad. She had always had an edge on her, especially whenever there were people listening.

—Miss Hill, don't you see these ladies are waiting?

—Look lively, Miss Hill, please.

She would not cry many tears at leaving the Stores.

But in her new home, in a distant unknown country, it would not be like that. Then she would be married—she, Eveline. People would treat her with respect then. She would not be treated as her mother had been. Even now, though she was over nineteen, she sometimes felt herself in danger of her father's violence. She knew it was that that had given her the palpitations. When they were growing up he had never gone for her, like he used to go for Harry and Ernest, because she was a girl; but latterly he had begun to threaten her and say what he would do to her only for her dead mother's sake. And now she had nobody to protect her. Ernest was dead and Harry, who was in the church decorating business, was nearly always down somewhere in the country. Besides, the invariable squabble for money on Saturday nights had begun to weary her unspeakably. She always gave her entire wages—seven shillings—and Harry always sent up what he could but the trouble was to get any money from her father. He said she used to squander the money, that she had no head, that he wasn't going to give her his hard-earned money to throw about the streets, and much more, for he was usually fairly bad of a Saturday night. In the end he would give her the money and ask her had she any intention of buying Sunday's dinner. Then she had to rush out as quickly as she could and do her marketing, holding her black leather purse tightly in her hand as she elbowed her way through the crowds and returning home late under her load of provisions. She had hard work to keep the house together and to see that the two young children who had been left to her charge went to school regularly and got their meals regularly. It was hard work—a hard life—but now that she was about to leave it she did not find it a wholly undesirable life.

She was about to explore another life with Frank. Frank was very kind, manly, open-hearted. She was to go away with him by the night-boat to be his wife and to live with him in Buenos Ayres where he had a home waiting for her. How well she remembered the first time she had seen him; he was lodging in a house on the main road where she used to visit. It seemed a few weeks ago. He was standing at the gate, his peaked cap pushed back on his head and his hair tumbled forward over a face of bronze. Then they had come to know each other. He used to meet her outside the Stores every evening and see her home. He took her to see *The Bohemian Girl* and she felt elated as she sat in an unaccustomed part of the theatre with him. He was awfully fond of music and sang a little. People knew that they were courting and, when he sang about the lass that loves a sailor, she always felt pleasantly confused. He used to call her Poppens out of fun. First of all it had been an excitement for her to have a fellow and then she had begun to like him. He had tales of distant countries. He had started as a deck boy at a pound a month on a ship of the Allan Line going out to Canada. He told her the names of the ships he had been on and the names of the different services. He had sailed through the Straits of Magellan and he told her stories of the terrible Patagonians. He had fallen on his feet in Buenos Ayres, he said, and had come over to the old country just for a holiday. Of course, her father had found out the affair and had forbidden her to have anything to say to him.

—I know these sailor chaps, he said.

One day he had quarrelled with Frank and after that she had to meet her lover secretly.

The evening deepened in the avenue. The white of two letters in her lap grew indistinct. One was to Harry; the other was to her father. Ernest had been her favorite but she liked Harry too. Her father was becoming old lately, she noticed; he would miss her. Sometimes he could be very nice. Not long before, when she had been laid up for a day, he had read her out a ghost story and made toast for her at the fire. Another day, when their mother was alive, they had all gone for a picnic to the Hill of Howth. She remembered her father putting on her mother's bonnet to make the children laugh.

Her time was running out but she continued to sit by the window, leaning her head against the window curtain, inhaling the odor of dusty cretonne. Down far in the avenue she could hear a street organ playing. She knew the air. Strange that it should come that very night to remind her of the promise to her mother, her promise to keep the home together as long as she could. She remembered the last night of her mother's illness; she was again in the close dark room at the other side of the hall and outside she heard a melancholy air of Italy. The organ-player had been ordered to go away and given sixpence. She remembered her father strutting back into the sickroom saying:

—Damned Italians! coming over here!

As she mused, the pitiful vision of her mother's life laid its spell on the very quick of her being—that life of commonplace sacrifices closing in final craziness. She trembled as she heard again her mother's voice saying constantly with foolish insistence:

—Derevaun Seraun! Derevaun Seraun!

She stood up in a sudden impulse of terror. Escape! She must escape! Frank would save her. He would give her life, perhaps love, too. But she wanted to live. Why should she be unhappy? She had a right to happiness. Frank would take her in his arms, fold her in his arms. He would save her.

She stood among the swaying crowd in the station at the North Wall. He held her hand and she knew that he was speaking to her, saying something about the passage over and over again. The station was full of soldiers with brown baggages. Through the wide doors of the sheds she caught a glimpse of the black mass of the boat, lying in beside the quay wall, with illumined portholes. She answered nothing. She felt her cheek pale and cold and, out of a maze of distress, she prayed to God to direct her, to show her what was her duty. The boat blew a long mournful whistle into the mist. If she went, tomorrow she would be on the sea with Frank, steaming towards Buenos Ayres. Their passage had been booked. Could she still draw back after all he had done for her? Her distress awoke a nausea in her body and she kept moving her lips in silent fervent prayer.

A bell clanged upon her heart. She felt him seize her hand:

—Come!

All the seas of the world tumbled about her heart.

He was drawing her into them: he would drown her. She gripped with both hands at the iron railing.

—Come!

No! No! No! It was impossible. Her hands clutched the iron in frenzy. Amid the seas she sent a cry of anguish!

—Eveline! Evvy!

He rushed beyond the barrier and called to her to follow. He was shouted at to go on but he still called to her. She set her white face to him, passive, like a helpless animal. Her eyes gave him no sign of love or farewell or recognition.

D. H. LAWRENCE

# A Sick Collier

SHE WAS TOO GOOD for him, everybody said. Yet still she did not regret marrying him. He had come courting her when he was only nineteen, and she twenty. He was in build what they call a tight little fellow; short, dark, with a warm color, and that upright set of the head and chest, that flaunting way in movement recalling a mating bird, which denotes a body taut and compact with life. Being a good worker he had earned decent money in the mine, and having a good home had saved a little.

She was a cook at "Uplands," a tall, fair girl, very quiet. Having seen her walk down the street, Horsepool had followed her from a distance. He was taken with her, he did not drink, and he was not lazy. So, although he seemed a bit simple, without much intelligence, but having a sort of physical brightness, she considered, and accepted him.

When they were married they went to live in Scargill Street, in a highly respectable six-roomed house which they had furnished between them. The street was built up the side of a long, steep hill. It was narrow and rather tunnel-like. Nevertheless, the back looked out over the adjoining pasture, across a wide valley of fields and woods, in the bottom of which the mine lay snugly.

He made himself gaffer in his own house. She was unacquainted with a collier's mode of life. They were married on a Saturday. On the Sunday night he said:

"Set th' table for my breakfast, an' put my pit-things afront o' th' fire. I s'll be gettin' up at ha'ef pas' five. Tha nedna shift thysen not till when ter likes."

He showed her how to put a newspaper on the table for a cloth. When she demurred:

"I want none o' your white cloths i' th' mornin'. I like ter be able to slobber if I feel like it," he said.

He put before the fire his moleskin trousers, a clean singlet, or sleeveless vest of thick flannel, a pair of stockings and his pit-boots, arranging them all to be warm and ready for morning.

"Now tha sees. That wants doin' ivery night."

Punctually at half-past five he left her, without any form of leave-taking, going downstairs in his shirt.

When he arrived home at four o'clock in the afternoon his dinner was ready to be dished up. She was startled when he came in, a short, sturdy figure, with a face indescribably black and streaked. She stood before the fire in her white blouse and white apron, a fair girl, the picture of beautiful cleanliness. He "clommaxed" in, in his heavy boots.

"Well, how 'as ter gone on?" he asked.

"I was ready for you to come home," she replied tenderly. In his black face the whites of his brown eyes flashed at her.

"An' I wor ready for comin'," he said. He planked his tin bottle and snap-bag on the dresser, took off his coat and scarf and waistcoat, dragged his arm-chair nearer the fire and sat down.

"Let's ha'e a bit o' dinner, then, Lucy—I'm about clammed," he said.

"Aren't you goin' to wash yourself first?"

"What am I to wesh mysen for?"

"Well, you can't eat your dinner—"

"Oh, strike a daisy, Missis! Dunna I eat my snap i' th' pit wi'out weshin'?—forced to."

She served the dinner and sat opposite him. His small bullet head was quite black, save for the whites of his eyes and his scarlet lips. It gave her a queer sensation to see him open his red mouth and bare his white teeth as he ate. His arms and hands were mottled black; his bare, strong neck got a little fairer as it settled towards his shoulders, reassuring her. There was the faint indescribable odor of the pit in the room, an odor of damp, exhausted air.

"Why is your vest so black on the shoulders?" she asked.

"My singlet? That's wi' th' watter droppin' on us from th' roof. This is a dry un as I put on afore I come up. They ha'e gre't clothes-'osses, an' as we change us things, we put 'em on theer ter dry."

When he washed himself, kneeling on the hearth-rug stripped to the waist, she felt afraid of him again. He was so muscular, he seemed so intent on what he was doing, so intensely himself, like a vigorous animal. And as he stood wiping himself, with his naked breast towards her, she felt rather sick, seeing his thick arms bulge their muscles.

They were nevertheless very happy. He was at a great pitch of pride because of her. The men in the pit might chaff him, they might try to entice him away, but nothing could reduce his self-assured pride because of her, nothing could unsettle his almost infantile satisfaction. In the evening he sat in his arm-chair chattering to her, or listening as she read the newspaper to him. When it was fine, he would go into the street, squat on his heels as colliers do, with his back against the wall of his parlor, and call to the passers-by, in greeting, one after another. If no one were passing, he was content just to squat and smoke, having such a fund of sufficiency and satisfaction in his heart. He was well married.

They had not been wed a year when all Brent and Wellwood's men came out on strike. Willy was in the Union, so with a pinch they scrambled through. The furniture was not all paid for, and other debts were incurred. She worried and contrived, he left it to her. But he was a good husband; he gave her all he had.

The men were out fifteen weeks. They had been back just over a year when Willy had an accident in the mine, tearing his bladder. At the pit head the doctor talked of the hospital. Losing his head entirely, the young collier raved like a madman, what with pain and fear of hospital.

"Tha s'lt go whoam, Willy, tha s'lt go whoam," the deputy said.

A lad warned the wife to have the bed ready. Without speaking or hesitating she prepared. But when the ambulance came, and she heard him shout with pain at being moved, she was afraid lest she should sink down. They carried him in.

"Yo' should 'a' had a bed i' th' parlor, Missis," said the deputy, "then we shouldna' ha' had to hawkse 'im upstairs, an' it 'ud 'a' saved your legs."

But it was too late now. They got him upstairs.

"They let me lie, Lucy," he was crying, "they let me lie two mortal hours on th' sleck afore they took me outer th' stall. Th' peen, Lucy, th' peen; oh, Lucy, th' peen, th' peen!"

"I know th' pain's bad, Willy, I know. But you must try an' bear it a bit."

"Tha manna carry on in that form, lad, thy missis 'll niver be able ter stan' it." said the deputy.

"I canna 'elp it, it's the peen, it's th' peen," he cried again. He had never been ill in his life. When he had smashed a finger he could look at the wound. But this pain came from inside, and terrified him. At last he was soothed and exhausted.

It was some time before she could undress him and wash him. He would let no other woman do for him, having that savage modesty usual in such men.

For six weeks he was in bed, suffering much pain. The doctors were not quite sure what was the matter with him, and scarcely knew what to do. He could eat, he did not lose flesh, nor strength, yet the pain continued, and he could hardly walk at all.

In the sixth week the men came out in the national strike. He would get up quite early in the morning and sit by the window. On Wednesday, the second week of the strike, he sat gazing out on the street as usual, a bullet-headed young man, still vigorous-looking, but with a peculiar expression of hunted fear in his face.

"Lucy," he called, "Lucy!"

She, pale and worn, ran upstairs at his bidding.

"Gi'e me a han'kercher," he said.

"Why, you've got one," she replied, coming near.

"Tha nedna touch me," he cried. Feeling his pocket, he produced a white handkerchief.

"I non want a white un, gi'e me a red un," he said.

"An' if anybody comes to see you," she answered, giving him a red handkerchief.

"Besides," she continued, "you needn't ha' brought me upstairs for that."

"I b'lieve th' peen's commin' on again," he said, with a little horror in his voice.

"It isn't, you know it isn't," she replied. "The doctor says you imagine it's there when it isn't."

"Canna I feel what's inside me?" he shouted.

"There's a traction-engine coming downhill," she said. "That'll scatter them.—I'll just go an' finish your pudding."

She left him. The traction-engine went by, shaking the houses. Then the street was quiet, save for the men. A gang of youths from fifteen to twenty-five years old were playing marbles in the middle of the road. Other little groups of men were playing on the pavement. The street was gloomy. Willy could hear the endless calling and shouting of men's voices.

"Tha'rt skinchin'!"

"I arena!"

"Come 'ere with that blood-alley."

"Swop us four for't."

"Shonna, gie's hold on't."

He wanted to be out, he wanted to be playing marbles. The pain had weakened his mind, so that he hardly knew any self-control.

Presently another gang of men lounged up the

street. It was pay morning. The Union was paying the men in the Primitive Chapel. They were returning with their half-sovereigns.

"Sorry!" bawled a voice. "Sorry!"

The word is a form of address, corruption probably of "Sirrah." Willy started almost out of his chair.

"Sorry!" again bawled a great voice. "Art goin' wi' me to see Notts play Villa?"

Many of the marble-players started up.

"What time is it? There's no treens, we s'll ha'e ter walk."

The street was alive with men.

"Who's goin' ter Nottingham ter see th' match?" shouted the same big voice. A very large, tipsy man, with his cap over his eye, was calling.

"Com' on—aye, com' on!" came many voices. The street was full of the shouting of men. They split up in excited cliques and groups.

"Play up, Notts!" the big man shouted.

"Plee up, Notts!" shouted the youths and men. They were at kindling pitch. It only needed a shout to rouse them. Of this the careful authorities were aware.

"I'm goin', I'm goin'!" shouted the sick man at his window.

Lucy came running upstairs.

"I'm goin' ter see Notts play Villa on th' Meadows ground," he declared.

"You—*you* can't go. There are no trains. You can't walk nine miles."

"I'm goin' ter see th' match," he declared, rising.

"You know you can't. Sit down now an' be quiet."

She put her hand on him. He shook it off.

"Leave me alone, leave me alone. It's thee as ma'es th' peen come, it's thee. I'm goin' ter Nottingham to see th' football match."

"Sit down—folks'll hear you, and what will they think?"

"Come off'n me. Com' off. It's her, it's her as does it. Com' off."

He seized hold of her. His little head was bristling with madness, and he was strong as a lion.

"Oh, Willy!" she cried.

"It's 'er, it's 'er. Kill her!" he shouted, "kill 'er."

"Willy, folks'll hear you."

"Th' peen's commin' on again, I tell yer. I'll kill her for it."

He was completely out of his mind. She struggled with him to prevent his going to the stairs. When she escaped from him, who was shouting and raving, she beckoned to her neighbor, a girl of twenty-four, who was cleaning the window across the road.

Ethel Mellor was the daughter of a well-to-do check-weighman. She ran across in fear to Mrs. Horsepool. Hearing the man raving, people were running out in the street and listening. Ethel hurried upstairs. Everything was clean and pretty in the young home.

Willy was staggering round the room, after the slowly retreating Lucy, shouting:

"Kill her! Kill her!"

"Mr. Horsepool!" cried Ethel, leaning against the bed, white as the sheets, and trembling. "Whatever are you saying?"

"I tell yer it's 'er fault as th' peen comes on—I tell yer it is! Kill 'er—kill 'er!"

"Kill Mrs. Horsepool!" cried the trembling girl. "Why, you're ever so fond of her, you know you are."

"The peen—I ha'e such a lot o' peen—I want to kill 'er."

He was subsiding. When he sat down his wife collapsed in a chair, weeping noiselessly. The tears ran down Ethel's face. He sat staring out of the window; then the old, hurt look came on his face.

"What 'ave I been sayin'?" he asked, looking piteously at his wife.

"Why!" said Ethel, "you've been carrying on something awful, saying: 'Kill her, kill her!' "

"Have I, Lucy?" he faltered.

"You didn't know what you were saying," said his young wife gently but coldly.

His face puckered up. He bit his lips, then broke into tears, sobbing uncontrollably, with his face to the window.

There was no sound in the room but of three people crying bitterly, breath caught in sobs. Suddenly Lucy put away her tears and went over to him.

"You didn't know what you was sayin', Willy. I know you didn't. I knew you didn't, all the time. It doesn't matter, Willy. Only don't do it again."

In a little while, when they were calmer, she went downstairs with Ethel.

"See if anybody is looking in the street," she said.

Ethel went into the parlor and peeped through the curtains.

"Aye!" she said. "You may back your life Lena an' Mrs. Severn'll be out gorping, and that clat-fartin' Mrs. Allsop."

"Oh, I hope they haven't heard anything! If it gets about as he's out of his mind, they'll stop his compensation, I know they will."

"They'd never stop his compensation for *that,*" protested Ethel.

"Well, they *have* been stopping—"

"It'll not get about. I s'll tell nobody."

"Oh, but if it does, whatever shall we do . . . ?"

## LUIGI PIRANDELLO

# The Soft Touch of Grass

THEY WENT into the next room, where he was sleeping in a big chair, to ask if he wanted to look at her for the last time before the lid was put on the coffin.

"It's dark. What time is it?" he asked.

It was nine-thirty in the morning, but the day was overcast and the light dim. The funeral had been set for ten o'clock.

Signor Pardi stared up at them with dull eyes. It hardly seemed possible that he could have slept so long and well all night. He was still numb with sleep and the sorrow of these last days. He would have liked to cover his face with his hands to shut out the faces of his neighbors grouped about his chair in the thin light; but sleep had weighted his body like lead, and although there was a tingling in his toes urging him to rise, it quickly went away. Should he still give way to his grief? He happened to say aloud, "Always . . ." but he said it like someone settling himself under the covers to go back to sleep. They all looked at him questioningly. Always what?

Always dark, even in the daytime, he had wanted to say, but it made no sense. The day after her death, the day of her funeral, he would always remember this wan light and his deep sleep, too, with her lying dead in the next room. Perhaps the windows. . . .

"The windows?"

Yes, they were still closed. They had not been opened during the night, and the warm glow of those big dripping candles lingered. The bed had been taken away and she was there in her padded casket, rigid and ashen against the creamy satin.

No. Enough. He had seen her.

He closed his eyes, for they burned from all the crying he had done these past few days. Enough. He had slept and everything had been washed away with that sleep. Now he was relaxed, with a sense of sorrowful emptiness. Let the casket be closed and carried away with all it held of his past life.

But since she was still there. . . .

He jumped to his feet and tottered. They caught him and, with eyes still closed, he allowed himself to be led to the open casket. When he opened his eyes and saw her, he called her by name, her name that lived for him alone, the name in which he saw her and knew her in all the fullness of the life they had shared together. He glared resentfully at the others daring to stare at her lying still in death. What did they know about her? They could not even imagine what it meant to him to be deprived of her. He felt like screaming, and it must have been apparent, for his son hurried over to take him away. He was quick to see the meaning of this and felt a chill as though he were stripped bare. For shame—those foolish ideas up to the very last, even after his night-long sleep. Now they must hurry so as not to keep the friends waiting who had come to follow the coffin to the church.

"Come on, Papa. Be reasonable."

With angry, piteous eyes, the bereaved man turned back to his big chair.

Reasonable, yes; it was useless to cry out the anguish that welled within him and that could never be expressed by words or deeds. For a husband who is left a widower at a certain age, a man still yearning for his wife, can the loss be the same as that of a son for whom—at a certain point—it is almost timely to be left an orphan? Timely, since he was on the point of getting married and would, as soon as the three months' mourning were passed, now that he had the added excuse that it was better for both of them to have a woman to look after the house.

"Pardi! Pardi!" they shouted from the entrance hall.

His chill became more intense when he understood clearly for the first time that they were not calling him but his son. From now on their surname would belong more to his son than to him. And he, like a fool, had gone in there to cry out the living name of his mate, like a profanation. For shame! Yes, useless, foolish ideas, he now realized, after that long sleep which had washed him clean of everything.

Now the one vital thing to keep him going was his curiosity as to how their new home would be arranged. Where, for example, were they going to have him sleep? The big double bed had been removed. Would he have a small bed? he wondered. Yes, probably his son's single bed. Now he would have the small bed. And his son would soon be lying in a big bed, his wife beside him within arm's reach. He, alone, in his little bed, would stretch out his arms into thin air.

He felt torpid, perplexed, with a sensation of emptiness inside and all around him. His body was numb from sitting so long. If he tried now to get up he felt sure that he would rise light as a feather in all that emptiness, now that his life was reduced to nothing. There was hardly any difference between himself and the big chair. Yet that chair appeared secure on its four legs, whereas he no longer knew where his feet and legs belonged nor what to do with his hands. What did he care about his life? He did not care particularly about the lives of others, either. Yet as he was still alive he must go on. Begin again—some sort of life which he could not yet conceive and which he certainly would never have contemplated if things had not changed in his own world. Now, deposed like this all of a sudden, not old and yet no longer young. . . .

He smiled and shrugged his shoulders. For his son, all at once, he had become a child. But after all, as everyone knows, fathers are children to their grown sons who are full of worldly ambition and have successfully outdistanced them in positions of importance. They keep their fathers in idleness to repay all they have received when they themselves were small, and their fathers in turn become young again.

The single bed. . . .

But they did not even give him the little room where his son had slept. Instead, they said, he would feel more independent in another, almost hidden on the courtyard; he would feel free there to do as he liked. They refurnished it with all the best pieces, so it would not occur to anyone that it had once been a servant's room. After the marriage, all the front rooms were pretentiously decorated and newly furnished, even to the luxury of carpets. Not a trace remained of the way the old house had looked. Even with his own furniture relegated to that little dark room, out of the mainstream of the young people's existence, he did not feel at home. Yet, oddly enough, he did not resent the disregard he seemed to have reaped along with the old furniture, because he admired the new rooms and was satisfied with his son's success.

But there was another deeper reason, not too clear as yet, a promise of another life, all shining and colorful, which was erasing the memory of the old one. He even drew a secret hope from it that a new life might begin for him too. Unconsciously, he sensed the luminous opening of a door at his back whence he might escape at the right moment, easy enough now that no one bothered about him, leaving him as if on holiday in the sanctuary of his little room "to do as he pleased." He felt lighter than air. His eyes had a gleam in them that colored everything, leading him from marvel to marvel, as though he really were a child again. He had the eyes of a child—lively and open wide on a world which was still new.

He took the habit of going out early in the morning to begin his holiday which was to last as long as his life lasted. Relieved of all responsibilities, he agreed to pay his son so much every month out of his pension for his maintenance. It was very little. Though he needed nothing, his son thought he should keep some money for himself to satisfy any need he might have. But need for what? He was satisfied now just to look on at life.

Having shaken off the weight of experience, he no longer knew how to get along with oldsters. He avoided them. And the younger people considered him too old, so he went to the park where the children played.

That was how he started his new life—in the meadow among the children in the grass. What an exhilarating scent the grass had, and so fresh where it grew thick and high. The children played hide-and-seek there. The constant trickle of some hidden stream outpurled the rustle of the leaves. Forgetting their game, the children pulled off their shoes and stockings. What a delicious feeling to sink into all that freshness of soft new grass with bare feet!

He took off one shoe and was stealthily removing the other when a young girl appeared before him, her face flaming. "You pig!" she cried, her eyes flashing.

Her dress was caught up in front on a bush, and she quickly pulled it down over her legs, because he was looking up at her from where he sat on the ground.

He was stunned. What had she imagined? Already she had disappeared. He had wanted to enjoy the children's innocent fun. Bending down, he put his two hands over his hard, bare feet. What had she seen wrong? Was he too old to share a child's delight in going barefoot in the grass? Must one immediately think evil because he was old? Ah, he knew that he could change in a flash from being a child to becoming a man again, if he must. He was still a man, after all, but he didn't want to think about it. He refused to think about it. It was really as a child that he had taken off his shoes. How wrong it was of that wretched girl to insult him like that! He threw himself face down on the grass. All his grief, his loss, his daily loneliness had brought about this gesture, interpreted now in the light of vulgar malice. His gorge rose in disgust and bitterness. Stupid girl! If he had wanted that—even his son admitted he might have "some desires"—he had plenty of money in his pocket for such needs.

Indignant, he pulled himself upright. Shamefacedly, with trembling hands, he put on his shoes again. All the blood had gone to his head and the pulse now beat hot behind his eyes. Yes, he knew where to go for that. He knew.

Calmer now, he got up and went back to the house. In the welter of furniture which seemed to have been placed there on purpose to drive him mad, he threw himself on the bed and turned his face to the wall.

*Translated by Lily Duplaix*

FRANZ KAFKA

# The Hunter Gracchus

TWO BOYS were sitting on the harbor wall playing with dice. A man was reading a newspaper on the steps of the monument, resting in the shadow of a hero who was flourishing his sword on high. A girl was filling her bucket at the fountain. A fruit-seller was lying beside his wares, gazing at the lake. Through the vacant window and door openings of a café one could see two men quite at the back drinking their wine. The proprietor was sitting at a table in front and dozing. A bark was silently making for the little harbor, as if borne by invisible means over the water. A man in a blue blouse climbed ashore and drew the rope through a ring. Behind the boatman two other men in dark coats with silver buttons carried a bier, on which, beneath a great flower-patterned fringed silk cloth, a man was apparently lying.

Nobody on the quay troubled about the newcomers; even when they lowered the bier to wait for the boatman, who was still occupied with his rope, nobody went nearer, nobody asked them a question, nobody accorded them an inquisitive glance.

The pilot was still further detained by a woman who, a child at her breast, now appeared with loosened hair on the deck of the boat. Then he advanced and indicated a yellowish two-storied house that rose abruptly on the left near the water; the bearers took up their burden and bore it to the low but gracefully pillared door. A little boy opened a window just in time to see the party vanishing into the house, then hastily shut the window again. The door too was now shut; it was of black oak, and very strongly made. A flock of doves which had been flying around the belfry alighted in the street before the house. As if their food were stored within, they assembled in front of the door. One of them flew up to the first story and pecked at the window-pane. They were bright-hued, well-tended, lively birds. The woman on the boat flung grain to them in a wide sweep; they ate it up and flew across to the woman.

A man in a top hat tied with a band of black crêpe now descended one of the narrow and very steep lanes that led to the harbor. He glanced around vigilantly, everything seemed to distress him, his mouth twisted at the sight of some offal in a corner. Fruit skins were lying on the steps of the monument; he swept them off in passing with his stick. He rapped at the house door, at the same time taking his top hat from his head with his black-gloved hand. The door was opened at once, and some fifty little boys appeared in two rows in the long entry hall, and bowed to him.

The boatman descended the stairs, greeted the gentleman in black, conducted him up to the first story, led him around the bright and elegant loggia which encircled the courtyard, and both of them entered, while the boys pressed after them at a respectful distance, a cool spacious room looking toward the back, from whose window no habitation, but only a bare, blackish-gray rocky wall was to be seen. The bearers were busied in setting up and lighting several long candles at the head of the bier, yet these did not give light, but only disturbed the shadows which had been immobile till then, and made them flicker over the walls. The cloth covering the bier had been thrown back. Lying on it was a man with wildly matted hair, who looked somewhat like a hunter. He lay without motion and, it seemed, without breathing, his eyes closed; yet only his trappings indicated that this man was probably dead.

The gentleman stepped up to the bier, laid his hand on the brow of the man lying upon it, then kneeled down and prayed. The boatman made a sign to the bearers to leave the room; they went out, drove away the boys who had gathered outside, and shut the door. But even that did not seem to satisfy the gentleman, he glanced at the boatman; the boatman understood, and vanished through a side door into the next room. At once the man on the bier opened his eyes, turned his face painfully toward the gentleman, and said: "Who are you?" Without any mark of surprise the gentleman rose from his kneeling posture and answered: "The Burgomaster of Riva."

The man on the bier nodded, indicated a chair with a feeble movement of his arm, and said, after the Burgomaster had accepted his invitation: "I knew that, of course, Burgomaster, but in the first moments of returning consciousness I always forget, everything goes around before my eyes, and it is best to ask about anything even if I know. You too probably know that I am the Hunter Gracchus."

"Certainly," said the Burgomaster. "Your arrival was announced to me during the night. We had been asleep for a good while. Then toward midnight my wife cried: 'Salvatore'—that's my name—'look at that dove at the window.' It was really a dove, but as big as a cock. It flew over me and said in my ear: 'Tomorrow the dead Hunter Gracchus is coming; receive him in the name of the city.' "

The Hunter nodded and licked his lips with the tip of his tongue: "Yes, the doves flew here before me. But do you believe, Burgomaster, that I shall remain in Riva?"

"I cannot say that yet," replied the Burgomaster. "Are you dead?"

"Yes," said the Hunter, "as you see. Many years ago, yes, it must be a great many years ago, I fell from a precipice in the Black Forest—that is in Germany—when I was hunting a chamois. Since then I have been dead."

"But you are alive too." said the Burgomaster.

"In a certain sense," said the Hunter, "in a certain sense I am alive too. My death ship lost its way; a wrong turn of the wheel, a moment's absence of mind on the pilot's part, the distraction of my lovely native country, I cannot tell what it was; I only know this, that I remained on earth and that ever since my ship has sailed earthly waters. So I, who asked for nothing better than to live among my mountains, travel after my death through all the lands of the earth."

"And you have no part in the other world?" asked the Burgomaster, knitting his brow.

"I am forever," replied the Hunter, "on the great stair that leads up to it. On that infinitely wide and spacious stair I clamber about, sometimes up, sometimes down, sometimes on the right, sometimes on the left, always in motion. The Hunter has been turned into a butterfly. Do not laugh."

"I am not laughing," said the Burgomaster in self-defense.

"That is very good of you," said the Hunter. "I am always in motion. But when I make a supreme flight and see the gate actually shining before me I awaken presently on my old ship, still stranded forlornly in some earthly sea or other. The fundamental error of my onetime death grins at me as I lie in my cabin. Julia, the wife of the pilot, knocks at the door and brings me on my bier the morning drink of the land whose coasts we chance to be passing. I lie on a wooden pallet, I wear—it cannot be a pleasure to look at me—a filthy winding sheet, my hair and beard, black tinged with gray, have grown together inextricably, my limbs are covered with a great flowered-patterned woman's shawl with long fringes. A sacramental candle stands at my head and lights me. On the wall opposite me is a little picture, evidently of a bushman who is aiming his spear at me and taking cover as best he can behind a beautifully painted shield. On shipboard one often comes across silly pictures, but that is the silliest of them all. Otherwise my wooden cage is quite empty. Through a hole in the side the warm airs of the southern night come in, and I hear the water slapping against the old boat.

"I have lain here ever since the time when, as the Hunter Gracchus living in the Black Forest, I followed a chamois and fell from a precipice. Everything happened in good order. I pursued, I fell, bled to death in a ravine, died, and this ship should have conveyed me to the next world. I can still remember how gladly I stretched myself out on this pallet for the first time. Never did the mountains listen to such songs from me as these shadowy walls did then.

"I had been glad to live and I was glad to die. Before I stepped aboard, I joyfully flung away my wretched load of ammunition, my knapsack, my hunting rifle that I had always been proud to carry, and I slipped into my winding sheet like a girl into her marriage dress. I lay and waited. Then came the mishap."

"A terrible fate," said the Burgomaster, raising his hand defensively. "And you bear no blame for it?"

"None," said the Hunter. "I was a hunter; was there any sin in that? I followed my calling as a hunter in the Black Forest, where there were still wolves in those days. I lay in ambush, shot, hit my mark, flayed the skins from my victims: was there any sin in that? My labors were blessed. 'The Great Hunter of the Black Forest' was the name I was given. Was there any sin in that?"

"I am not called upon to decide that," said the Burgomaster, "but to me also there seems to be no sin in such things. But then, whose is the guilt?"

"The boatman's," said the Hunter. "Nobody will read what I say here, no one will come to help me; even if all the people were commanded to help me, every door and window would remain shut, everybody would take to bed and draw the bed-clothes over his head, the whole earth would become an inn for the night. And there is sense in that, for nobody knows of me, and if anyone knew he would not know where I could be found, and if he knew where I could be found, he would not know how to deal with me, he would not know how to help me. The thought of helping me is an illness that has to be cured by taking to one's bed.

"I know that, and so I do not shout to summon help, even though at moments—when I lose control over myself, as I have done just now, for instance—I think seriously of it. But to drive out such thoughts I need only look around me and verify where I am, and—I can safely assert—have been for hundreds of years."

"Extraordinary," said the Burgomaster, "extraordinary. And now do you think of staying here in Riva with us?"

"I think not," said the Hunter with a smile, and, to excuse himself, he laid his hand on the Burgomaster's knee. "I am here, more than that I do not know, further than that I cannot go. My ship has no rudder, and it is driven by the wind that blows in the undermost regions of death."

*Translated by Willa and Edwin Muir*

## FRANZ KAFKA

# First Sorrow

A TRAPEZE ARTIST—this art, practiced high in the vaulted domes of the great variety theaters, is admittedly one of the most difficult humanity can achieve—had so arranged his life that, as long as he kept working in the same building, he never came down from his trapeze by night or day, at first only from a desire to perfect his skill, but later because custom was too strong for him. All his needs, very modest needs at that, were supplied by relays of attendants who watched from below and sent up and hauled down again in specially constructed containers whatever he required. This way of living caused no particular inconvenience to the theatrical people, except that, when other turns were on the stage, his being still up aloft, which could not be dissembled, proved somewhat distracting, as also the fact that, although at such times he mostly kept very still, he drew a stray glance here and there from the public. Yet the management overlooked this, because he was an extraordinary and unique artist. And of course they recognized that this mode of life was no mere prank, and that only in this way could he really keep himself in constant practice and his art at the pitch of its perfection.

Besides, it was quite healthful up there, and when in the warmer seasons of the year the side windows all around the dome of the theater were thrown open and sun and fresh air came pouring irresistibly into the dusky vault, it was even beautiful. True, his social life was somewhat limited, only sometimes a fellow acrobat swarmed up the ladder to him, and then they both sat on the trapeze, leaning left and right against the supporting ropes, and chatted, or builders' workmen repairing the roof exchanged a few words with him through an open window, or the fireman, inspecting the emergency lighting in the top gallery, called over to him something that sounded respectful but could hardly be made out. Otherwise nothing disturbed his seclusion; occasionally, perhaps, some theater hand straying through the empty theater of an afternoon gazed thoughtfully up into the great height of the roof, almost beyond eyeshot, where the trapeze artist, unaware that he was being observed, practiced his art or rested.

The trapeze artist could have gone on living peacefully like that, had it not been for the inevitable journeys from place to place, which he found extremely trying. Of course his manager saw to it that his sufferings were not prolonged one moment more than necessary; for town travel, racing automobiles were used, which whirled him, by night if possible or in the earliest hours of the morning, through the empy streets at breakneck speed, too slow all the same for the trapeze artist's impatience; for railway journeys, a whole compartment was reserved, in which the trapeze artist, as a possible though wretched alternative to his usual way of living, could pass the time up on the luggage rack; in the next town on their circuit, long before he arrived, the trapeze was already slung up in the theater and all the doors leading to the stage were flung wide open, all corridors kept free—yet the manager never knew a happy moment until the trapeze artist set his foot on the rope ladder and in a twinkling, at long last, hung aloft on his trapeze.

Despite so many journeys having been successfully arranged by the manager, each new one embarrassed him again, for the journeys, apart from everything else, got on the nerves of the artist a great deal.

Once when they were again traveling together, the trapeze artist lying on the luggage rack dreaming, the manager leaning back in the opposite window seat reading a book, the trapeze artist addressed his companion in a low voice. The manager was immediately all attention. The trapeze artist, biting his lips, said that he must always in future have two trapezes for his performance instead of only one, two trapezes opposite each other. The manager at once agreed. But the trapeze artist, as if to show that the manager's consent counted for as little as his refusal, said that never again would he perform on only one trapeze, in no circumstances whatever. The very idea that it might happen at all seemed to make him shudder. The manager, watchfully feeling his way, once more emphasized his entire agreement, two trapezes were better than one, besides it would be an advantage to have a second bar, more variety could be introduced into the performance. At that the trapeze artist suddenly burst into tears. Deeply distressed, the manager sprang to his feet and asked what was the matter, then getting no answer climbed up on the seat and caressed him, cheek to cheek, so that his own face was bedabbled by the trapeze artist's tears. Yet it took much questioning and soothing endearment until the trapeze artist sobbed: "Only the one bar in my hands—how can I go on living!" That made it somewhat easier for the manager to comfort him; he promised to wire from the very next station for a second trapeze to be installed in the first town on their circuit; reproached himself for having let the artist work so long on only one trapeze; and thanked and praised him warmly for having at last brought the mistake to his notice. And so he succeeded in reassuring the trapeze artist, little by little, and was able to go back to his corner. But he himself was far from reassured, with deep uneasiness he kept glancing secretly at the trapeze artist over the top of his book. Once such ideas began to torment him, would they ever quite leave him alone? Would they not rather increase in urgency? Would they not threaten his very existence? And indeed the manager believed he could see, during the apparently peaceful sleep which had succeeded the fit of tears, the first furrows of care engraving themselves upon the trapeze artist's smooth, childlike forehead.

*Translated by Willa and Edwin Muir*

## SHERWOOD ANDERSON

# The Untold Lie

RAY PEARSON and Hal Winters were farm hands employed on a farm three miles north of Winesburg. On Saturday afternoons they came into town and wandered about through the streets with other fellows from the country.

Ray was a quiet, rather nervous man of perhaps fifty with a brown beard and shoulders rounded by too much and too hard labor. In his nature he was as unlike Hal Winters as two men can be unlike.

Ray was an altogether serious man and had a little sharp-featured wife who had also a sharp voice. The two, with half a dozen thin-legged children, lived in a tumble-down frame house beside a creek at the back end of the Wills farm where Ray was employed.

Hal Winters, his fellow employee, was a young fellow. He was not of the Ned Winters family, who were very respectable people in Winesburg, but was one of the three sons of the old man called Windpeter Winters who had a sawmill near Unionville, six miles away, and who was looked upon by everyone in Winesburg as a confirmed old reprobate.

People from the part of Northern Ohio in which Winesburg lies will remember old Windpeter by his unusual and tragic death. He got drunk one evening in town and started to drive home to Unionville along the railroad tracks. Henry Brattenburg, the butcher, who lived out that way, stopped him at the edge of the town and told him he was sure to meet the down train but Windpeter slashed at him with his whip and drove on. When the train struck and killed him and his two horses a farmer and his wife who were driving home along a nearby road saw the accident. They said that old Windpeter stood upon the seat of his wagon, raving and swearing at the onrushing locomotive, and that he fairly screamed with delight when the team, maddened by his incessant slashing at them, rushed straight ahead to certain death. Boys like young George Willard and Seth Richmond will remember the incident quite vividly because, although everyone in our town said that the old man would go straight to hell and that the community was better off without him, they had a secret conviction that he knew what he was doing and admired his foolish courage. Most boys have seasons of wishing they could die gloriously instead of just being grocery clerks and going on with their humdrum lives.

But this is not the story of Windpeter Winters nor yet of his son Hal who worked on the Wills farm with Ray Pearson. It is Ray's story. It will, however, be necessary to talk a little of young Hal so that you will get into the spirit of it.

Hal was a bad one. Everyone said that. There were three of the Winters boys in that family, John, Hal, and Edward, all broad-shouldered big fellows like old Windpeter himself and all fighters and woman-chasers and generally all-around bad ones.

Hal was the worst of the lot and always up to some devilment. He once stole a load of boards from his father's mill and sold them in Winesburg. With the money he bought himself a suit of cheap, flashy clothes. Then he got drunk and when his father came raving into town to find him, they met and fought with their fists on Main Street and were arrested and put into jail together.

Hal went to work on the Wills farm because there was a country school teacher out that way who had taken his fancy. He was only twenty-two then but had already been in two or three of what were spoken of in Winesburg as "women scrapes." Everyone who heard of his infatuation for the school teacher was sure it would turn out badly. "He'll only get her into trouble, you'll see," was the word that went around.

And so these two men, Ray and Hal, were at work in a field on a day in the late October. They were husking corn and occasionally something was said and they laughed. Then came silence. Ray, who was the more sensitive and always minded things more, had chapped hands and they hurt. He put them into his coat pockets and looked away across the fields. He was in a sad, distracted mood and was affected by the beauty of the country. If you knew the Winesburg country in the fall and how the low hills are splashed with yellows and reds you would understand his feeling. He began to think of the time, long ago when he was a young fellow living with his father, then a baker in Winesburg, and how on such days he had wandered away to the woods to gather nuts, hunt rabbits, or just to loaf about and smoke his pipe. His marriage had come about through one of his days of wandering. He had induced a girl who waited on trade in his father's shop to go with him and something had happened. He was thinking of that afternoon and how it had affected his whole life when a spirit of protest awoke in him. He had forgotten about Hal and muttered words. "Tricked by Gad, that's what I was, tricked by life and made a fool of," he said in a low voice.

As though understanding his thoughts, Hal Winters spoke up. "Well, has it been worth while? What about it, eh? What about marriage and all that?" he asked and then laughed. Hal tried to keep on laughing but he too was in an earnest mood. He began to talk earnestly. "Has a fellow got to do it?" he asked. "Has he got to be harnessed up and driven through life like a horse?"

Hal didn't wait for an answer but sprang to his feet and began to walk back and forth between the corn shocks. He was getting more and more excited. Bending down suddenly he picked up an ear of the yellow corn and threw it at the fence. "I've got Nell Gunther in trouble," he said. "I'm telling you, but you keep your mouth shut."

Ray Pearson arose and stood staring. He was almost a foot shorter than Hal, and when the younger man came and put his two hands on the older man's shoulders they made a picture. There they stood in the big empty field with the quiet corn shocks standing in rows behind them and the red and yellow hills in the distance, and from being just two indifferent workmen they had become all alive to each other. Hal sensed it and because that was his way he laughed. "Well, old daddy," he said awkwardly, "come on, advise me. I've got Nell in trouble. Perhaps you've been in the same fix yourself. I know what everyone would say is the right thing to do, but what do you say? Shall I marry and settle down? Shall I put myself into the harness to be worn out like an old horse? You know me, Ray. There can't anyone break me but I can break myself. Shall I do it or shall I tell Nell to go to the devil? Come on, you tell me. Whatever you say, Ray, I'll do."

Ray couldn't answer. He shook Hal's hands loose and turning walked straight away toward the barn. He was a sensitive man and there were tears in his eyes. He knew there was only one thing to say to Hal Winters, son of old Windpeter Winters, only one thing that all his own training and all the beliefs of the people he knew would approve, but for his life he couldn't say what he knew he should say.

At half-past four that afternoon Ray was puttering about the barnyard when his wife came up the lane along the creek and called him. After the talk with Hal he hadn't returned to the cornfield but worked about the barn. He had already done the evening chores and had seen Hal, dressed and ready for a roistering night in town, come out of the farmhouse and go into the road. Along the path to his own house he trudged behind his wife, looking at the ground and thinking. He couldn't make out what was wrong. Every time he raised his eyes and saw the beauty of the country in the failing light he wanted to do something he had never done before, shout or scream or hit his wife with his fists or something equally unexpected and terrifying. Along the path he went scratching his head and trying to make it out. He looked hard at his wife's back but she seemed all right.

She only wanted him to go into town for groceries and as soon as she had told him what she wanted began to scold. "You're always puttering," she said. "Now I want you to hustle. There isn't anything in the house for supper and you've got to get to town and back in a hurry."

Ray went into his own house and took an overcoat from a hook back of the door. It was torn about the pockets and the collar was shiny. His wife went into the bedroom and presently came out with a soiled cloth in one hand and three silver dollars in the other. Somewhere in the house a child wept bitterly and a dog that had been sleeping by the stove arose and yawned. Again the wife scolded. "The children will cry and cry. Why are you always puttering?" she asked.

Ray went out of the house and climbed the fence into a field. It was just growing dark and the scene that lay before him was lovely. All the low hills were washed with color and even the little clusters of bushes in the corners by the fences were alive with beauty. The whole world seemed to Ray Pearson to have become alive with something just as he and Hal had suddenly become alive when they stood in the cornfield staring into each other's eyes.

The beauty of the country about Winesburg was too much for Ray on that fall evening. That is all there was to it. He could not stand it. Of a sudden he forgot all about being a quiet old farm hand and throwing off the torn overcoat began to run across the field. As he ran he shouted a protest against his life, against all life, against everything that makes life ugly. "There was no promise made," he cried into the empty spaces that lay about him. "I didn't promise my Minnie anything and Hal hasn't made any promise to Nell. I know he hasn't. She went into the woods with him because she wanted to go. What he wanted she wanted. Why should I pay? Why should Hal pay? Why should anyone pay? I don't want Hal to become old and worn out. I'll tell him. I won't let it go on. I'll catch Hal before he gets to town and I'll tell him."

Ray ran clumsily and once he stumbled and fell down. "I must catch Hal and tell him," he kept thinking, and although his breath came in gasps he kept running harder and harder. As he ran he thought of things that hadn't come into his mind for years—how at the time he married he had planned to go west to his uncle in Portland, Oregon—how he hadn't wanted to be a farm hand, but had thought when he got out West he would go to sea and be a sailor or get a job on a ranch and ride a horse into Western towns, shouting and laughing and waking the people in the houses with his wild cries. Then as he ran he remembered his children and in fancy felt their hands clutching at him. All of his thoughts of himself were involved with the thoughts of Hal and he thought the children were clutching at the younger man also. "They are the accidents of life, Hal," he cried. "They are not mine or yours. I had nothing to do with them."

Darkness began to spread over the fields as Ray Pearson ran on and on. His breath came in little sobs. When he came to the fence at the edge of the road and confronted Hal Winters, all dressed up and smoking a pipe as he walked jauntily along, he could not have told what he thought or what he wanted.

Ray Pearson lost his nerve and this is really the end of the story of what happened to him. It was almost dark when he got to the fence and he put his hands on the top bar and stood staring. Hal Winters jumped a ditch and coming up close to Ray put his hands into his pockets and laughed. He seemed to have lost his own sense of what had happened in the cornfield and when he put up a strong hand and took hold of the lapel of Ray's coat he shook the old man as he might have shaken a dog that had misbehaved.

"You came to tell me, eh?" he said. "Well, never mind telling me anything. I'm not a coward and I've already made up my mind." He laughed again and jumped back across the ditch. "Nell ain't no fool," he said. "She didn't ask me to marry her. I want to marry her. I want to settle down and have kids."

Ray Pearson also laughed. He felt like laughing at himself and all the world.

As the form of Hal Winters disappeared in the dusk that lay over the road that led to Winesburg, he turned and walked slowly back across the fields to where he had left his torn overcoat. As he went some memory of pleasant evenings spent with the thin-legged children in the tumble-down house by the creek must have come into his mind, for he muttered words. "It's just as well. Whatever I told him would have been a lie," he said softly, and then his form also disappeared into the darkness of the fields.

## SHERWOOD ANDERSON

# Paper Pills

HE WAS AN OLD MAN with a white beard and huge nose and hands. Long before the time during which we will know him, he was a doctor and drove a jaded white horse from house to house through the streets of Winesburg. Later he married a girl who had money. She had been left a large fertile farm when her father died. The girl was quiet, tall, and dark, and to many people she seemed very beautiful. Everyone in Winesburg wondered why she married the doctor. Within a year after the marriage she died.

The knuckles of the doctor's hands were extraordinarily large. When the hands were closed they looked like clusters of unpainted wooden balls as large as walnuts fastened together by steel rods. He smoked a cob pipe and after his wife's death sat all day in his empty office close by a window that was covered with cobwebs. He never opened the window. Once on a hot day in August he tried but found it stuck fast and after that he forgot all about it.

Winesburg had forgotten the old man, but in Doctor Reefy there were the seeds of something very fine. Alone in his musty office in the Heffner Block above the Paris Dry Goods Company's store, he worked ceaselessly, building up something that he himself destroyed. Little pyramids of truth he erected and after erecting knocked them down again that he might have the truths to erect other pyramids.

Doctor Reefy was a tall man who had worn one

suit of clothes for ten years. It was frayed at the sleeves and little holes had appeared at the knees and elbows. In the office he wore also a linen duster with huge pockets into which he continually stuffed scraps of paper. After some weeks the scraps of paper became little hard round balls, and when the pockets were filled he dumped them out upon the floor. For ten years he had but one friend, another old man named John Spaniard who owned a tree nursery. Sometimes, in a playful mood, old Doctor Reefy took from his pockets a handful of the paper balls and threw them at the nursery man. "That is to confound you, you blithering old sentimentalist," he cried, shaking with laughter.

The story of Doctor Reefy and his courtship of the tall dark girl who became his wife and left her money to him was a very curious story. It is delicious, like the twisted little apples that grow in the orchards of Winesburg. In the fall one walks in the orchards and the ground is hard with frost underfoot. The apples have been taken from the trees by the pickers. They have been put in barrels and shipped to the cities where they will be eaten in apartments that are filled with books, magazines, furniture, and people. On the trees are only a few gnarled apples that the pickers have rejected. They look like the knuckles of Doctor Reefy's hands. One nibbles at them and they are delicious. Into a little round place at the side of the apple has been gathered all of its sweetness. One runs from tree to tree over the frosted ground picking the gnarled, twisted apples and filling his pockets with them. Only the few know the sweetness of the twisted apples.

The girl and Doctor Reefy began their courtship on a summer afternoon. He was forty-five then and already he had begun the practice of filling his pockets with the scraps of paper that became hard balls and were thrown away. The habit had been formed as he sat in his buggy behind the jaded white horse and went slowly along country roads. On the papers were written thoughts, ends of thoughts, beginnings of thoughts.

One by one the mind of Doctor Reefy had made the thoughts. Out of many of them he formed a truth that arose gigantic in his mind. The truth clouded the world. It became terrible and then faded away and the little thoughts began again.

The tall dark girl came to see Doctor Reefy because she was in the family way and had become frightened. She was in that condition because of a series of circumstances also curious.

The death of her father and mother and the rich acres of land that had come down to her had set a train of suitors on her heels. For two years she saw suitors almost every evening. Except two they were all alike. They talked to her of passion and there was a strained eager quality in their voices and in their eyes when they looked at her. The two who were different were much unlike each other. One of them, a slender young man with white hands, the son of a jeweler in Winesburg, talked continually of virginity. When he was with her he was never off the subject. The other, a black-haired boy with large ears, said nothing at all but always managed to get her into the darkness, where he began to kiss her.

For a time the tall dark girl thought she would marry the jeweler's son. For hours she sat in silence listening as he talked to her and then she began to be afraid of something. Beneath his talk of virginity she began to think there was a lust greater than in all the others. At times it seemed to her that as he talked he was holding her body in his hands. She imagined him turning it slowly about in the white hands and staring at it. At night she dreamed that he had bitten into her body and that his jaws were dripping. She had the dream three times, then she became in the family way to the one who said nothing at all but who in the moment of his passion actually did bite her shoulder so that for days the marks of his teeth showed.

After the tall dark girl came to know Doctor

Reefy it seemed to her that she never wanted to leave him again. She went into his office one morning and without her saying anything he seemed to know what had happened to her.

In the office of the doctor there was a woman, the wife of the man who kept the bookstore in Winesburg. Like all old-fashioned country practitioners, Doctor Reefy pulled teeth, and the woman who waited held a handkerchief to her teeth and groaned. Her husband was with her and when the tooth was taken out they both screamed and blood ran down on the woman's white dress. The tall dark girl did not pay any attention. When the woman and the man had gone the doctor smiled. "I will take you driving into the country with me," he said.

For several weeks the tall dark girl and the doctor were together almost every day. The condition that had brought her to him passed in an illness, but she was like one who has discovered the sweetness of the twisted apples, she could not get her mind fixed again upon the round perfect fruit that is eaten in the city apartments. In the fall after the beginning of her acquaintanceship with him she married Doctor Reefy and in the following spring she died. During the winter he read to her all of the odds and ends of thoughts he had scribbled on the bits of paper. After he had read them he laughed and stuffed them away in his pockets to become round hard balls.

ERNEST HEMINGWAY

# A Clean, Well-Lighted Place

IT WAS LATE and every one had left the café except an old man who sat in the shadow the leaves of the tree made against the electric light. In the day time the street was dusty, but at night the dew settled the dust and the old man liked to sit late because he was deaf and now at night it was quiet and he felt the difference. The two waiters inside the café knew that the old man was a little drunk, and while he was a good client they knew that if he became too drunk he would leave without paying, so they kept watch on him.

"Last week he tried to commit suicide," one waiter said.

"Why?"

"He was in despair."

"What about?"

"Nothing."

"How do you know it was nothing?"

"He has plenty of money."

They sat together at a table that was close against the wall near the door of the café and looked at the terrace where the tables were all empty except where the old man sat in the shadow of the leaves of the tree that moved slightly in the wind. A girl and a soldier went by in the street. The street light shone on the brass number on his collar. The girl wore no head covering and hurried beside him.

"The guard will pick him up," one waiter said.

"What does it matter if he gets what he's after?"

"He had better get off the street now. The guard will get him. They went by five minutes ago."

The old man sitting in the shadow rapped on his saucer with his glass. The younger waiter went over to him.

"What do you want?"

The old man looked at him. "Another brandy," he said.

"You'll be drunk," the waiter said. The old man looked at him. The waiter went away.

"He'll stay all night," he said to his colleague. "I'm sleepy now. I never get into bed before three o'clock. He should have killed himself last week."

The waiter took the brandy bottle and another saucer from the counter inside the café and marched out to the old man's table. He put down the saucer and poured the glass full of brandy.

"You should have killed yourself last week," he said to the deaf man. The old man motioned with his finger. "A little more," he said. The waiter poured on into the glass so that the brandy slopped over and ran down the stem into the top saucer of the pile. "Thank you," the old man said. The waiter took the bottle back inside the café. He sat down at the table with his colleague again.

"He's drunk now," he said.

"He's drunk every night."

"What did he want to kill himself for?"

"How should I know."

"How did he do it?"

"He hung himself with a rope."

"Who cut him down?"

"His niece."

"Why did they do it?"

"Fear for his soul."

"How much money has he got?"

"He's got plenty."

"He must be eighty years old."

"Anyway I should say he was eighty."

"I wish he would go home. I never get to bed

before three o'clock. What kind of hour is that to go to bed?"

"He stays up because he likes it."

"He's lonely. I'm not lonely. I have a wife waiting in bed for me."

"He had a wife once too."

"A wife would be no good to him now."

"You can't tell. He might be better with a wife."

"His niece looks after him. You said she cut him down."

"I know."

"I wouldn't want to be that old. An old man is a nasty thing."

"Not always. This old man is clean. He drinks without spilling. Even now, drunk. Look at him."

"I don't want to look at him. I wish he would go home. He has no regard for those who must work."

The old man looked from his glass across the square, then over at the waiters.

"Another brandy," he said, pointing to his glass. The waiter who was in a hurry came over.

"Finished," he said, speaking with that omission of syntax stupid people employ when talking to drunken people or foreigners. "No more tonight. Close now."

"Another," said the old man.

"No. Finished." The waiter wiped the edge of the table with a towel and shook his head.

The old man stood up, slowly counted the saucers, took a leather coin purse from his pocket and paid for the drinks, leaving half a peseta tip.

The waiter watched him go down the street, a very old man walking unsteadily but with dignity.

"Why didn't you let him stay and drink?" the unhurried waiter asked. They were putting up the shutters. "It is not half-past two."

"I want to go home to bed."

"What is an hour?'

"More to me than to him."

"An hour is the same."

"You talk like an old man yourself. He can buy a bottle and drink at home."

"It's not the same."

"No, it is not," agreed the waiter with a wife. He did not wish to be unjust. He was only in a hurry.

"And you? You have no fear of going home before your usual hour?"

"Are you trying to insult me?"

"No, hombre, only to make a joke."

"No," the waiter who was in a hurry said, rising from pulling down the metal shutters. "I have confidence. I am all confidence."

"You have youth, confidence, and a job," the older waiter said. "You have everything."

"And what do you lack?"

"Everything but work."

"You have everything I have."

"No. I have never had confidence and I am not young."

"Come on. Stop talking nonsense and lock up."

"I am of those who like to stay late at the café." the older waiter said. "With all those who do not want to go to bed. With all those who need a light for the night."

"I want to go home and into bed."

"We are of two different kinds," the older waiter said. He was now dressed to go home. "It is not only a question of youth and confidence although those things are very beautiful. Each night I am reluctant to close up because there may be some one who needs the café."

"Hombre, there are bodegas open all night long."

"You do not understand. This is a clean and pleasant café. It is well lighted. The light is very good and also, now, there are shadows of the leaves."

"Good night," said the younger waiter.

"Good night," the other said. Turning off the electric light he continued the conversation with himself. It is the light of course but it is necessary that the place be clean and pleasant. You do not want music. Certainly you do not want music. Nor can you stand before a bar with dignity although that is all that is provided for these hours. What did he fear? It was not fear or dread. It was a nothing that he knew too well. It was all a nothing and a man was nothing too. It was only that and light was all it needed and a certain cleanness and order. Some lived in it and never felt it but he knew it all was nada y pues nada y nada y pues nada. Our nada who art in nada, nada by the name thy kingdom nada thy will be nada in nada as it is in nada. Give us this nada our daily nada and nada us our nada as we nada our nadas and nada us not into nada but deliver us from nada; pues nada. Hail nothing full of nothing, nothing is with thee. He smiled and stood before a bar with a shining steam pressure coffee machine.

"What's yours?" asked the barman.

"Nada."

"Otro loco más," said the barman and turned away.

"A little cup," said the waiter.

The barman poured it for him.

"The light is very bright and pleasant but the bar is unpolished," the waiter said.

The barman looked at him but did not answer. It was too late at night for conversation.

"You want another copita?" the barman asked.

"No, thank you," said the waiter and went out. He disliked bars and bodegas. A clean, well-lighted café was a very different thing. Now, without thinking further, he would go home to his room. He would lie in the bed and finally, with daylight, he would go to sleep. After all, he said to himself, it is probably only insomnia. Many must have it.

## GIUSEPPE DI LAMPEDUSA

# Joy and the Law

WHEN HE GOT onto the bus he irritated everyone. The briefcase crammed with other people's business, the enormous parcel which made his left arm stick out, the grey velvet scarf, the umbrella on the point of opening, all made it difficult for him to produce his return ticket. He was forced to put his parcel on the ticket collector's bench, setting off an avalanche of small coins; as he tried to bend down to pick them up, he provoked protests from those who stood behind him, who feared that because of his dallying their coats would be caught in the automatic doors. At last he managed to squeeze into the row of people clinging to the handles in the gangway. He was slight of build, but his bundles gave him the cubic capacity of a nun in seven habits. As the bus slid through the chaos of the traffic, his inconvenient bulk spread resentment from front to rear of the coach. He stepped on people's feet, they trod on his; he invited rebuke, and when he heard the word *cornuto* from the rear of the bus alluding to his presumed marital disgrace, his sense of honor compelled him to turn his head in that direction and make his exhausted eyes assume what he imagined to be a threatening expression.

The bus, meanwhile, was passing through streets where rustic baroque fronts hid a wretched hinterland which emerged at each street corner in the yellow light of eighty-year-old shops.

At his stop he rang the bell, descended, tripped

over the umbrella, and found himself alone at last on his square meter of disconnected footpath. He hastened to make sure that he still had his plastic wallet. And then he was free to relish his bliss.

Enclosed in that wallet were 37,245 lire—the "thirteenth monthly salary" received as a Christmas bonus an hour before. This sum meant the removal of several thorns from his flesh: the obligations to his landlord, all the more pressing because his was a controlled rent and he owed two quarters; and to the ever-punctual installment collector for the short lapin coat ("It suits you better than a long coat, my dear—it makes you look slimmer"); the dirty looks from the fishmonger and the greengrocer. Those four bank notes of high denomination also eased the fear of the next electricity bill, the pained glances at the children's shoes, and the anxious watching of the gas cylinder's flickering flame; they did not represent opulence, certainly, but did give that breathing space in distress which is the true joy of the poor; a couple of thousand lire might survive for a while, before being eaten up in the resplendence of a Christmas dinner.

However, he had known too many "thirteenths" to attribute the euphoria which now enveloped him to the ephemeral exhilaration they could produce. He was filled with a rosy feeling, as rosy as the wrapping on the sweet burden that was making his left arm numb. The feeling sprang from the seven-kilo Christmas cake, the panettone that he had brought home from the office. He had no passion for the mixture—as highly guaranteed as it was questionable—of flour, sugar, dried eggs and raisins. At heart he did not care for it at all. But seven kilos of luxury food all at once! A limited but vast abundance in a household where provisions came in hectograms and half-liters! A famous product in a larder devoted to third-rate items! What a joy for Maria! What a riot for the children who for two weeks would explore the unknown Wild West of an afternoon snack!

These, however, were the joys of others, the material joys of vanilla essence and colored cardboard; of panettone, in sum. His personal joy was different—a spiritual bliss based on pride and loving affection; yes, spiritual!

When, a few hours before, the baronet who was managing director of his firm had distributed pay envelopes and Christmas wishes with the overbearing affability of the pompous old man that he was, he also announced that the seven-kilo panettone, which had come with the compliments of the big firm that produced it, would be awarded to the most deserving employee; and he asked his dear colleagues democratically (that was the word he had actually used) to choose the lucky man then and there.

The panettone had stood on the middle of the desk, heavy, hermetically sealed, "laden with good omens" as the same baronet, dressed in Fascist uniform, would have said in Mussolini's phrase twenty years before. There was laughing and whispering among the employees; and then everyone, the managing director first, shouted his name. A great satisfaction; a guarantee that he would keep his job—in short, a triumph. Nothing that followed could lessen the tonic effect; neither the three hundred lire that he had to pay in the coffee bar below, treating his friends in the two-fold dusk of a squally sunset and dim neon lights, nor the weight of his trophy, nor the unpleasant comments in the bus—nothing; not even the lightning flash from the depths of his consciousness that it had all been an act of rather condescending pity from his fellow-employees: he was really too poor to permit the weed of pride to sprout where it had no business to appear.

He turned toward home across a decrepit street to which the bombardments of fifteen years previously had given the finishing touches, and finally reached the grim little square in the depths of which the ghostly edifice in which he lived stood tucked away.

He heartily greeted Cosimo, the porter, who despised him because he knew that his salary was lower than his own. Nine steps, three steps, nine steps: the floor where Cavaliere Tizio lived. Pooh! He did have a Fiat 1100, true enough, but he also had an old, ugly and dissolute wife. Nine steps, three steps—a slip almost made him fall—nine steps: young Sempronio's apartment; worse still!—a bone-idle lad, mad on Lambrettas and Vespas, whose hall was still unfurnished. Nine steps, three steps, nine steps: his own apartment, the little abode of a beloved, honest and honored man, a prize-winner, a bookkeeper beyond compare.

He opened the door and entered the narrow hall, already filled with the heavy smell of onion soup. He placed the weighty parcel, the briefcase loaded with other people's affairs, and his muffler on a little locker the size of a hamper. His voice rang out: "Maria! Come quickly! Come and see—what a beauty!"

His wife came out of the kitchen in a blue housecoat spotted with grime from saucepans; her little hands, still red from washing up, rested on a belly deformed by pregnancies. The children with their slimy noses crowded around the rose-colored sight and squealed without daring to touch it.

"Oh good! Did you bring your pay back? I haven't a single lira left."

"Here it is, dear. I'll only keep the small change—245 lire. But look at this grace of God here!"

Maria had been pretty; until a few years previously she had had a cheeky little face and whimsical eyes. But the wrangles with the shopkeepers had made her voice grow harsh, the poor food had ruined her complexion, the incessant peering into a future clouded with problems had spent the luster of her eyes. Only the soul of a saint survived within her, inflexible and bereft of tenderness; deep-seated virtue expressing itself in rebukes and restrictions; and in addition a repressed but persistent pride of class because she was the granddaughter of a big hatter in one of the main streets, and despised the origins of her Girolamo—whom she adored as a silly but beloved child—because they were inferior to her own.

Indifferently her eyes ran over the gilded cardboard box. "That's fine. Tomorrow we'll send it to Signor Risma, the solicitor; we're under such an obligation to him!"

Two years previously this solicitor had given him a complicated bookkeeping job to do, and over and above paying for it, had invited both of them to lunch in his abstract-and-metal apartment. The clerk had suffered acutely from the shoes bought specially for the occasion. And he and his Maria, his Andrea, his Saverio, his little Josephine were now to give up the only seam of abundance they had hit in many, many years, for that lawyer who had everything.

He ran to the kitchen, grabbed a knife, and rushed to cut the gold string that a deft working girl in Milan had beautifully tied around the wrapping paper; but a reddened hand wearily touched his shoulder. "Girolamo, don't behave like a child—you know we have to repay Risma's kindness."

The law had spoken: the law laid down by unblemished hat-shop owners.

"But dear, this is a prize, an award of merit, a token of esteem!"

"Don't say that. Nice people, those colleagues of yours, with their tender feelings! It was alms-giving, Giro, nothing but alms-giving." She called him by his old pet name, and smiled at him with eyes that only for him still held traces of the old spell. "Tomorrow I'll buy a little panettone, just big enough for us, and four of those twisted red candles from Standa's—that'll make it a fine feast!"

The next day he bought an undistinguished miniature panettone, and not four but two of the astonishing candles; through a delivery agency, at a cost of another two hundred lire, he forwarded the mammoth cake to the solicitor Risma.

After Christmas he had to buy a third panettone which, disguised by slicing, he took to his colleagues who were teasing him because they hadn't been offered a morsel of the sumptuous trophy.

A smoke screen enveloped the fate of the original cake. He went to the Lightning Delivery Agency to make enquiries. With disdain he was shown the receipts book which the solicitor's manservant had signed upside down. However, just after Twelfth Night a visiting card arrived "with sincerest thanks and best wishes."

Honor was saved.

*Translated by Alfred Alexander*

## KATHERINE ANNE PORTER

# Magic

AND, MADAME BLANCHARD, believe that I am happy to be here with you and your family because it is so serene, everything, and before this I worked for a long time in a fancy house—maybe you don't know what is a fancy house? Naturally . . . everyone must have heard sometime or other. Well, Madame, I work always where there is work to be had, and so in this place I worked very hard all hours, and saw too many things, things you wouldn't believe, and I wouldn't think of telling you, only maybe it will rest you while I brush your hair. You'll excuse me too but I could not help hearing you say to the laundress maybe someone had bewitched your linens, they fall away so fast in the wash. Well, there was a girl there in that house, a poor thing, thin, but well-liked by all the men who called, and you understand she could not get along with the woman who ran the house. They quarreled, the madam cheated her on her checks: you know, the girl got a check, a brass one, every time, and at the week's end she gave those back to the madam, yes, that was the way, and got her percentage, a very small little of her earnings: it is a business, you see, like any other—and the madam used to pretend the girl had given back only so many checks, you see, and really she had given many more, but after they were out of her hands, what could she do? So she would say, I will get out of this place, and curse and cry. Then the madam would hit her over the head. She always hit people over the head with bottles, it was the way she fought. My good heavens, Madame Blanchard, what confusion there would be sometimes with a girl running raving downstairs, and the madam pulling her back by the hair and smashing a bottle on her forehead.

It was nearly always about the money, the girls got in debt so, and if they wished to go they could not without paying every sou marqué. The madam had full understanding with the police; the girls must come back with them or go to the jails. Well, they always came back with the policemen or with another kind of man friend of the madam: she could make men work for her too, but she paid them very well for all, let me tell you: and so the girls stayed on unless they were sick; if so, if they got too sick, she sent them away again.

Madame Blanchard said, "You are pulling a little here," and eased a strand of hair: "and then what?"

Pardon—but this girl, there was a true hatred between her and the madam. She would say many times, I make more money than anybody else in the house, and every week were scenes. So at last she said one morning, Now I will leave this place, and she took out forty dollars from under her pillow and said, Here's your money! The madam began to shout, Where did you get all that, you—? and accused her of robbing the men who came to visit her. The girl said, Keep your hands off or I'll brain you: and at that the madam took hold of her shoulders, and began to lift her knee and kick this girl most terribly in the stomach, and even in her most secret place, Madame Blanchard, and then she beat her in the face with a bottle, and the girl fell back again into her room where I was making clean. I helped her to the bed, and she sat there holding her sides with her head hanging down, and when she got up again there was blood everywhere she had sat. So then the madam came in once more and screamed, Now you can get out, you are no good for me any more: I don't repeat all, you understand it is too much. But she took all the money she could find, and at the door she gave the girl a great push in the back with her knee, so that she fell again in the street, and then got up and went away with the dress barely on her.

After this the men who knew this girl kept saying, Where is Ninette? And they kept asking this in the next days, so that the madam could not say any longer, I put her out because she is a thief. No, she began to see she was wrong to send this Ninette away, and then she said, She will be back in a few days, don't trouble yourself.

And now, Madame Blanchard, if you wish to hear, I come to the strange part, the thing recalled to me when you said your linens were bewitched. For the cook in that place was a woman, colored like myself, like myself with much French blood just the same, like myself living always among people who worked spells. But she had a very hard heart, she helped the madam in everything, she liked to watch all that happened, and she gave away tales on the girls. The madam trusted her above everything, and she said, Well, where can I find that slut? because she had gone altogether out of Basin Street before the madam began to ask the police to bring her again. Well, the cook said, I know a charm that works here in New Orleans, colored women do it to bring back their men: in seven days they come again very happy to stay and they cannot say why: even your enemy will come back to you believing you are his friend. It is a New Orleans charm for sure, for certain, they say it does not work even across the river. . . . And then they did it just as the cook said. They took the chamber pot of this girl from under her bed, and in it they mixed with water and milk all the relics of her they found there: the hair from her brush, and the face powder from the puff, and even little bits of her nails they found about the edges of the carpet where she sat by habit to cut her finger- and toe-nails; and they dipped the sheets with her blood into the water, and all the time the cook said something over it in a low voice; I could not hear all, but at last she said to the madam, Now spit in it: and the madam spat, then the cook said, When she comes back she will be dirt under your feet.

Madame Blanchard closed her perfume bottle with a thin click: "Yes, and then?"

Then in seven nights the girl came back and she looked very sick, the same clothes and all, but happy to be there. One of the men said, Welcome home, Ninette! and when she started to speak to the madam, the madam said, Shut up and get upstairs and dress yourself. So Ninette, this girl, she said, I'll be down in just a minute. And after that she lived there quietly.

ISAAC BABEL

# The Death of Dolgushov

THE WAVES OF BATTLE rolled toward the town. At noon Korochayev sped past us in his black cloak; in disgrace, the commander of the Fourth Division fought alone, seeking death. Without breaking stride, he shouted to me, "Our communications are cut. Radzivillov and Brody are in flames!" and galloped away, his black cloak billowing, his pupils like coals.

On the plain, flat as a board, the brigades were forming up. The sun wheeled behind a gauze of purple dust. Wounded men were snatching a bite in the ditches. Nurses lay on the grass, singing under their breath. Afonka's scouts combed the fields looking for corpses and equipment. Afonka rode up to within two paces of me and, without turning his head, said, "They really clobbered us—no getting away from it! There's a feeling they may replace the division commander. The men are beginning to wonder. . . ."

The Poles had reached the woods about three versts from us and set up machine guns nearby. The whine and whistle of bullets filled the air, rising to an intolerable pitch. Bullets bit the earth, burrowing into it, squirming impatiently. Vytyagaichenko, the regiment commander, lay in the sun snoring. He cried out in his sleep and woke up. He mounted his horse and rode up to the lead squadron. His face was creased and red-streaked from his uncomfortable sleep, and his pockets were full of plums.

"Son of a bitch," he snarled and spat a pit from

his mouth. "Not again! Timoshka, raise the standard!"

"We're off then?" Timoshka asked, taking the staff out of the stirrups and unfurling the banner with a star on it and something or other about the Third International.

"We'll see," said Vytyagaichenko, and all of a sudden yelled out, "Mount up, boys! Squadron commanders muster your men!"

The buglers sounded the alert. The squadrons formed up into a column. One of the wounded climbed out of a ditch and, screening his face with his palm, spoke to Vytyagaichenko. "Taras Grigoryevich, I'm a delegate. It's beginning to look like we're getting left behind. . . ."

"You'll fight them off," Vytyagaichenko mumbled, making his horse rear.

"Well, it's like this, Taras Grigoryevich, we kind of get the feeling we won't fight them off!" said the wounded man, addressing Vytyagaichenko's retreating figure.

"Quit whining," Vytyagaichenko said back, over his shoulder. "I won't leave you, all right?" And he gave the order to move off.

At that very moment, Afonka Bida, my friend, chimed in with his plaintive, womanish voice. "Let's not start off at a trot, Taras Grigoryevich—it's a good five versts. How do you expect us to fight if our horses are dropping? What's all the rush, anyway—you afraid you won't get there in time for the Feast of the Virgin or something?"

"Walking pace!" Vytyagaichenko gave the command without raising his eyes. The regiment moved off.

"If it's true about the division commander," whispered Afonka, falling behind, "if they really replace him, then you can kiss your ass good-bye. Period." Tears welled up in his eyes. I gazed at Afonka in astonishment. He whirled round, grabbed his cap, cleared his throat, whooped, and shot off.

The two of us were left alone—just me and

Grishchuk with his stupid cart. We were buffeted back and forth between fire zones until evening. Division HQ had disappeared. No other units wanted to take us. The Poles reached Brody and were thrown back by a counterattack. We rode up to the town cemetery. A Polish patrol leapt out from behind the tombstones, raised their rifles, and started firing at us. Grishchuk turned around, all four wheels of his car screeching.

"Grishchuk!" I shouted through the screeching and the wind.

"Nothing to worry about," he replied gloomily.

"Our number's up," I screamed, gripped by the elation of mortal danger. "Our number's up, my friend!"

"What's the point of women taking such trouble?" he replied, more gloomily still. "What's the point of all the matchmaking, the weddings with all the old ladies having such a good time . . . ?"

A tail of pink flared in the sky and went out. The Milky Way came into view among the stars.

"It really kills me," said Grishchuk mournfully, pointing with his whip at a man sitting at the side of the road. "It kills me, the idea of women going to all that trouble. . . ."

The man sitting by the side of the road was Dolgushov, the telephone operator. His legs spread apart, he regarded us intently.

"The thing is," he said when we rode up, "I'm finished . . . get it?"

"Got it," replied Grishchuk, stopping the horses.

"You're going to have to use up a cartridge on me," said Dolgushov. He sat with his back against a tree. His boots stuck out in different directions. Without taking his eyes off me, he carefully rolled back his shirt. His belly had been ripped open, his guts had spilled onto his knees, and his heart could be seen beating. "Soon those Polack gents will be here—they'll have some fun with me. Here's my papers—you'll write my mother, tell her what happened. . . ."

"No," I said, and spurred my horse.

Dolgushov spread his blue palms on the ground, regarding them with disbelief. "You running off?" he mumbled, slipping down. "Run, you rat!"

A light sweat broke out over my body. The chatter of machine guns got faster, hysterical with intensity.

Haloed by the setting sun, Afonka Bida galloped up to us. "We're giving them something to think about," he shouted cheerfully. "What's all this here?"

I pointed to Dolgushov and rode off.

They spoke briefly—I didn't hear the words. Dolgushov handed his papers to the troop commander. Afonka slipped them into his boot and shot Dolgushov in the mouth.

"Afonka," I said, as I rode up to the Cossack, twisting my face into a smile, "I just couldn't."

"Get out of here," he replied, turning pale. "I'll kill you. You people with eyeglasses have about as much pity for our kind as a cat for a mouse!"

He cocked his rifle. I moved at a walk, not turning, feeling a deathly chill in my spine.

"Cut it out," shouted Grishchuk behind me. "That's enough fooling around." He grabbed Afonka's arm.

"That cringing yellowbelly!" Afonka shouted. "He won't get away from me!"

Grishchuk caught up with me at the turn. Afonka was out of sight. He had ridden off in the opposite direction.

"There, you see, Grishchuk," I said, "today I lost Afonka, my first friend."

Grishchuk took out a wrinkled apple from under the seat. "Eat!" he said, "eat it, please!"

*Translated by Stephen B. Pearl*

## MIKHAIL ZOSCHENKO

# The Bathhouse

OUR BATHHOUSES are not so bad. You can wash yourself. Only we have trouble in our bathhouses with the tickets. Last Saturday I went to a bathhouse, and they gave me two tickets. One for my linen, the other for my hat and coat.

But where is a naked man going to put tickets? To say it straight—no place. No pockets. Look around—all stomach and legs. The only trouble's with the tickets. Can't tie them to your beard.

Well, I tied a ticket to each leg so as not to lose them both at once. I went into the bath.

The tickets are flapping about on my legs now. Annoying to walk like that. But you've got to walk. Because you've got to have a bucket. Without a bucket, how can you wash? That's the only trouble.

I look for a bucket. I see one citizen washing himself with three buckets. He is standing in one, washing his head in another, and holding the third with his left hand so no one would take it away.

I pulled at the third bucket; among other things, I wanted to take it for myself. But the citizen won't let go.

"What are you up to," says he, "stealing other people's buckets?" As I pull, he says, "I'll give you a bucket between the eyes, then you won't be so damn happy."

I say: "This isn't the tsarist regime," I say, "to go around hitting people with buckets. Egotism," I say, "sheer egotism. Other people," I say, "have to wash themselves too. You're not in a theater," I say.

But he turned his back and starts washing himself again.

"I can't just stand around," think I, "waiting his pleasure. He's likely to go on washing himself," think I, "for another three days."

I moved along.

After an hour I see some old joker gaping around, no hands on his bucket. Looking for soap or just dreaming, I don't know. I just lifted his bucket and made off with it.

So now there's a bucket, but no place to sit down. And to wash standing—what kind of washing is that? That's the only trouble.

All right. So I'm standing. I'm holding the bucket in my hand and I'm washing myself.

But all around me everyone's scrubbing clothes like mad. One is washing his trousers, another's rubbing his drawers, a third's wringing something out. You no sooner get yourself all washed up than you've dirty again. They're splattering me, the bastards. And such a noise from all the scrubbing—it takes all the joy out of washing. You can't even hear where the soap squeaks. That's the only trouble.

"To hell with them," I think. "I'll finish washing at home."

I go back to the locker room. I give them one ticket, they give me my linen. I look. Everything's mine, but the trousers aren't mine.

"Citizens," I say, "mine didn't have a hole here. Mine had a hole over here."

But the attendant says: "We aren't here," he says, "just to watch for your holes. You're not in a theater," he says.

All right. I put these pants on, and I'm about to go get my coat. They won't give me my coat. They want the ticket. I'd forgotten the ticket on my leg. I had to undress. I took off my pants. I look for the ticket. No ticket. There's the string tied around my leg, but no ticket. The ticket had been washed away.

I give the attendant the string. He doesn't want it.

"You don't get anything for a string," he says. "Anybody can cut off a bit of string," he says. "Wouldn't be enough coats to go around. Wait," he says, "till everyone leaves. We'll give you what's left over."

I say: "Look here, brother, suppose there's nothing left but crud? This isn't a theater," I say. "I'll identify it for you. One pocket," I say, "is torn, and there's no other. As for the buttons," I say, "the top one's there, the rest are not to be seen."

Anyhow, he gave it to me. But he wouldn't take the string.

I dressed, and went out on the street. Suddenly I remembered: I forgot my soap.

I went back again. They won't let me in, in my coat.

"Undress," they say.

I say, "Look, citizens. I can't undress for the third time. This isn't a theater," I say. "At least give me what the soap costs."

Nothing doing.

Nothing doing—all right. I went without the soap.

Of course, the reader who is accustomed to formalities might be curious to know: what kind of a bathhouse was this? Where was it located? What was the address?

What kind of a bathhouse? The usual kind. Where it costs ten kopecks to get in.

*Translated by Sidney Monas*

## WILLIAM CARLOS WILLIAMS

# The Use of Force

THEY WERE new patients to me, all I had was the name, Olson. Please come down as soon as you can, my daughter is very sick.

When I arrived I was met by the mother, a big startled looking woman, very clean and apologetic who merely said, Is this the doctor? and let me in. In the back, she added. You must excuse us, doctor, we have her in the kitchen where it is warm. It is very damp here sometimes.

The child was fully dressed and sitting on her father's lap near the kitchen table. He tried to get up, but I motioned for him not to bother, took off my overcoat and started to look things over. I could see that they were all very nervous, eyeing me up and down distrustfully. As often, in such cases, they weren't telling me more than they had to, it was up to me to tell them; that's why they were spending three dollars on me.

The child was fairly eating me up with her cold, steady eyes, and no expression to her face whatever. She did not move and seemed, inwardly, quiet; an unusually attractive little thing, and as strong as a heifer in appearance. But her face was flushed, she was breathing rapidly, and I realized that she had a high fever. She had magnificent blonde hair, in profusion. One of those picture children often reproduced in advertising leaflets and the photogravure sections of the Sunday papers.

She's had a fever for three days, began the father

and we don't know what it comes from. My wife has given her things, you know, like people do, but it don't do no good. And there's been a lot of sickness around. So we tho't you'd better look her over and tell us what is the matter.

As doctors often do I took a trial shot at it as a point of departure. Has she had a sore throat?

Both parents answered me together, No . . . No, she says her throat don't hurt her.

Does your throat hurt you? added the mother to the child. But the little girl's expression didn't change nor did she move her eyes from my face.

Have you looked?

I tried to, said the mother, but I couldn't see.

As it happens we had been having a number of cases of diphtheria in the school to which this child went during that month and we were all, quite apparently, thinking of that, though no one had as yet spoken of the thing.

Well, I said, suppose we take a look at the throat first. I smiled in my best professional manner and asking for the child's first name I said, come on, Mathilda, open your mouth and let's take a look at your throat.

Nothing doing.

Aw, come on, I coaxed, just open your mouth wide and let me take a look. Look, I said opening both hands wide, I haven't anything in my hands. Just open up and let me see.

Such a nice man, put in the mother. Look how kind he is to you. Come on, do what he tells you to. He won't hurt you.

At that I ground my teeth in disgust. If only they wouldn't use the word "hurt" I might be able to get somewhere. But I did not allow myself to be hurried or disturbed but speaking quietly and slowly I approached the child again.

As I moved my chair a little nearer suddenly with one cat-like movement both her hands clawed instinctively for my eyes and she almost reached them too. In fact she knocked my glasses flying and they fell, though unbroken, several feet away from me on the kitchen floor.

Both the mother and father almost turned themselves inside out in embarrassment and apology. You bad girl, said the mother, taking her and shaking her by one arm. Look what you've done. The nice man. . . .

For heaven's sake, I broke in. Don't call me a nice man to her. I'm here to look at her throat on the chance that she might have diphtheria and possibly die of it. But that's nothing to her. Look here, I said to the child, we're going to look at your throat. You're old enough to understand what I'm saying. Will you open it now by yourself or shall we have to open it for you?

Not a move. Even her expression hadn't changed. Her breaths however were coming faster and faster. Then the battle began. I had to do it. I had to have a throat culture for her own protection. But first I told the parents that it was entirely up to them. I explained the danger but said that I would not insist on a throat examination so long as they would take the responsibility.

If you don't do what the doctor says you'll have to go to the hospital, the mother admonished her severely.

Oh yeah? I had to smile to myself. After all, I had already fallen in love with the savage brat, the parents were contemptible to me. In the ensuing struggle they grew more and more abject, crushed, exhausted while she surely rose to magnificent heights of insane fury of effort bred of her terror of me.

The father tried his best, and he was a big man but the fact that she was his daughter, his shame at her behavior and his dread of hurting her made him release her just at the critical moment several times when I had almost achieved success, till I wanted to kill him. But his dread also that she might have diphtheria made him tell me to go on, go on though he himself was almost fainting, while the mother moved back and forth behind us raising and lowering her hands in an agony of apprehension.

Put her in front of you on your lap, I ordered, and hold both her wrists.

But as soon as he did the child let out a scream. Don't, you're hurting me. Let go of my hands. Let them go I tell you. Then she shrieked terrifyingly, hysterically. Stop it! Stop it! You're killing me!

Do you think she can stand it, doctor! said the mother.

You get out, said the husband to his wife. Do you want her to die of diphtheria?

Come on now, hold her, I said.

Then I grasped the child's head with my left hand and tried to get the wooden tongue depressor between her teeth. She fought, with clenched teeth, desperately! But now I also had grown furious—at a child. I tried to hold myself down but I couldn't. I know how to expose a throat for inspection. And I did my best. When finally I got the wooden spatula behind the last teeth and just the point of it into the mouth cavity, she opened up for an instant but before I could see anything she came down again and gripping the wooden blade between her molars she reduced it to splinters before I could get it out again.

Aren't you ashamed, the mother yelled at her. Aren't you ashamed to act like that in front of the doctor?

Get me a smooth-handled spoon of some sort, I told the mother. We're going through with this. The child's mouth was already bleeding. Her tongue was cut and she was screaming in wild hysterical shrieks. Perhaps I should have desisted and come back in an hour or more. No doubt it would have been better. But I have seen at least two children lying dead in bed of neglect in such cases, and feeling that I must get a diagnosis now or never I went at it again. But the worst of it was that I too had got beyond reason. I could have torn the child apart in my own fury and enjoyed it. It was a pleasure to attack her. My face was burning with it.

The damned little brat must be protected against her own idiocy, one says to one's self at such times. Others must be protected against her. It is social necessity. And all these things are true. But a blind fury, a feeling of adult shame, bred of a longing for muscular release are the operatives. One goes on to the end.

In a final unreasoning assault I overpowered the child's neck and jaws. I forced the heavy silver spoon back of her teeth and down her throat till she gagged. And there it was—both tonsils covered with membrane. She had fought valiantly to keep me from knowing her secret. She had been hiding that sore throat for three days at least and lying to her parents in order to escape just such an outcome as this.

Now truly she *was* furious. She had been on the defensive before but now she attacked. Tried to get off her father's lap and fly at me while tears of defeat blinded her eyes.

## YUKIO MISHIMA

# Swaddling Clothes

HE WAS ALWAYS BUSY, Toshiko's husband. Even tonight he had to dash off to an appointment, leaving her to go home alone by taxi. But what else could a woman expect when she married an actor—an attractive one? No doubt she had been foolish to hope that he would spend the evening with her. And yet he must have known how she dreaded going back to their house, unhomely with its Western-style furniture and with the bloodstains still showing on the floor.

Toshiko had been oversensitive since girlhood: that was her nature. As the result of constant worrying she never put on weight, and now, an adult woman, she looked more like a transparent picture than a creature of flesh and blood. Her delicacy of spirit was evident to her most casual acquaintance.

Earlier that evening, when she had joined her husband at a night club, she had been shocked to find him entertaining friends with an account of "the incident." Sitting there in his American-style suit, puffing at a cigarette, he had seemed to her almost a stranger.

"It's a fantastic story," he was saying, gesturing flamboyantly as if in an attempt to outweigh the attractions of the dance band. "Here this new nurse for our baby arrives from the employment agency, and the very first thing I notice about her is her stomach. It's enormous—as if she had a pillow stuck under her kimono! No wonder, I thought, for I soon saw that she could eat more than the rest of us put together. She polished off the contents of our rice bin like that. . . ." He snapped his fingers. " 'Gastric dilation'—that's how she explained her girth and her appetite. Well, the day before yesterday we heard groans and moans coming from the nursery. We rushed in and found her squatting on the floor, holding her stomach in her two hands, and moaning like a cow. Next to her our baby lay in his cot, scared out of his wits and crying at the top of his lungs. A pretty scene, I can tell you!"

"So the cat was out of the bag?" suggested one of their friends, a film actor like Toshiko's husband.

"Indeed it was! And it gave me the shock of my life. You see, I'd completely swallowed that story about 'gastric dilation.' Well, I didn't waste any time. I rescued our good rug from the floor and spread a blanket for her to lie on. The whole time the girl was yelling like a stuck pig. By the time the doctor from the maternity clinic arrived, the baby had already been born. But our sitting room was a pretty shambles!"

"Oh, that I'm sure of!" said another of their friends, and the whole company burst into laughter.

Toshiko was dumbfounded to hear her husband discussing the horrifying happening as though it were no more than an amusing incident which they chanced to have witnessed. She shut her eyes for a moment and all at once she saw the newborn baby lying before her: on the parquet floor the infant lay, and his frail body was wrapped in bloodstained newspapers.

Toshiko was sure that the doctor had done the whole thing out of spite. As if to emphasize his scorn for this mother who had given birth to a bastard under such sordid conditions, he had told his assistant to wrap the baby in some loose newspapers, rather than proper swaddling. This callous treatment of the newborn child had offended Toshiko. Overcoming her disgust at the entire scene, she had fetched a brand-new piece of flannel from her cupboard and, having swaddled the baby in it, had lain him carefully in an armchair.

This all had taken place in the evening after her husband had left the house. Toshiko had told him nothing of it, fearing that he would think her oversoft, oversentimental; yet the scene had engraved itself deeply in her mind. Tonight she sat silently thinking back on it, while the jazz orchestra brayed and her husband chatted cheerfully with his friends. She knew that she would never forget the sight of the baby, wrapped in stained newspapers and lying on the floor—it was a scene fit for a butchershop. Toshiko, whose own life had been spent in solid comfort, poignantly felt the wretchedness of the illegitimate baby.

I am the only person to have witnessed its shame, the thought occurred to her. The mother never saw her child lying there in its newspaper wrappings, and the baby itself of course didn't know. I alone shall have to preserve that terrible scene in my memory. When the baby grows up and wants to find out about his birth, there will be no one to tell him, so long as I preserve silence. How strange that I should have this feeling of guilt! After all, it was I who took him up from the floor, swathed him properly in flannel, and laid him down to sleep in the armchair.

They left the night club and Toshiko stepped into the taxi that her husband had called for her. "Take this lady to Ushigomé," he told the driver and shut the door from the outside. Toshiko gazed through the window at her husband's smiling face and noticed his strong, white teeth. Then she leaned back in the seat, oppressed by the knowledge that their life together was in some way too easy, too painless. It would have been difficult for her to put her thoughts into words. Through the rear window of the taxi she took a last look at her husband. He was striding along the street toward his Nash car, and soon the back of his rather garish tweed coat had blended with the figures of the passers-by.

The taxi drove off, passed down a street dotted with bars and then by a theatre, in front of which the throngs of people jostled each other on the pavement. Although the performance had only just ended, the lights had already been turned out and in the half dark outside it was depressingly obvious that the cherry blossoms decorating the front of the threatre were merely scraps of white paper.

Even if that baby should grow up in ignorance of the secret of his birth, he can never become a respectable citizen, reflected Toshiko, pursuing the same train of thoughts. Those soiled newspaper swaddling clothes will be the symbol of his entire life. But why should I keep worrying about him so much? Is it because I feel uneasy about the future of my own child? Say twenty years from now, when our boy will have grown up into a fine, carefully educated young man, one day by a quirk of fate he meets the other boy, who then will also have turned twenty. And say that the other boy, who has been sinned against, savagely stabs him with a knife. . . .

It was a warm, overcast April night, but thoughts of the future made Toshiko feel cold and miserable. She shivered on the back seat of the car.

No, when the time comes I shall take my son's place, she told herself suddenly. Twenty years from now I shall be forty-three. I shall go to that young man and tell him straight out about everything—about his newspaper swaddling clothes, and about how I went and wrapped him in flannel.

The taxi ran along the dark wide road that was bordered by the park and by the Imperial Palace moat. In the distance Toshiko noticed the pinpricks of light which came from the blocks of tall office buildings.

Twenty years from now that wretched child will be in utter misery. He will be living a desolate, hopeless, poverty-stricken existence—a lonely rat. What else could happen to a baby who has had such a birth? He'll be wandering through the streets by himself, cursing his father, loathing his mother.

No doubt Toshiko derived a certain satisfaction from her somber thoughts: she tortured herself with them without cease. The taxi approached Hanzomon and drove past the compound of the British Embassy. At that point the famous rows of cherry trees were spread out before Toshiko in all their purity. On the spur of the moment she decided to go and view the blossoms by herself in the dark night. It was a strange decision for a timid and unadventurous young woman, but then she was in a strange state of mind and she dreaded the return home. That evening all sorts of unsettling fancies had burst open in her mind.

She crossed the wide street—a slim, solitary figure in the darkness. As a rule when she walked in the traffic Toshiko used to cling fearfully to her companion, but tonight she darted alone between the cars and a moment later had reached the long narrow park that borders the Palace moat. Chidorigafuchi, it is called—the Abyss of the Thousand Birds.

Tonight the whole park had become a grove of blossoming cherry trees. Under the calm cloudy sky the blossoms formed a mass of solid whiteness. The paper lanterns that hung from wires between the trees had been put out; in their place electric light bulbs, red, yellow, and green, shone dully beneath the blossoms. It was well past ten o'clock and most of the flower-viewers had gone home. As the occasional passers-by strolled through the park, they would automatically kick aside the empty bottles or crush the waste paper beneath their feet.

Newspapers, thought Toshiko, her mind going back once again to those happenings. Bloodstained newspapers. If a man were ever to hear of that piteous birth and know that it was he who had lain there, it would ruin his entire life. To think that I, a perfect stranger, should from now on have to keep such a secret—the secret of a man's whole existence. . . .

Lost in these thoughts, Toshiko walked on through the park. Most of the people still remaining there were quiet couples; no one paid her any attention. She noticed two people sitting on a stone bench beside the moat, not looking at the blossoms, but gazing silently at the water. Pitch black it was, and swathed in heavy shadows. Beyond the moat the somber forest of the Imperial Palace blocked her view. The trees reached up, to form a solid dark mass against the night sky. Toshiko walked slowly along the path beneath the blossoms hanging heavily overhead.

On a stone bench, slightly apart from the others, she noticed a pale object—not, as she had at first imagined, a pile of cherry blossoms, nor a garment forgotten by one of the visitors to the park. Only when she came closer did she see that it was a human form lying on the bench. Was it, she wondered, one of those miserable drunks often to be seen sleeping in public places? Obviously not, for the body had been systematically covered with newspapers, and it was the whiteness of those papers that had attracted Toshiko's attention. Standing by the bench, she gazed down at the sleeping figure.

It was a man in a brown jersey who lay there, curled up on layers of newspapers, other newspapers covering him. No doubt this had become his normal night residence now that spring had arrived. Toshiko gazed down at the man's dirty, unkempt hair, which in places had become hopelessly matted. As she observed the sleeping figure wrapped in its newspapers, she was inevitably reminded of the baby who had lain on the floor in its wretched swaddling clothes. The shoulder of the man's jersey rose and fell in the darkness in time with his heavy breathing.

It seemed to Toshiko that all her fears and premonitions had suddenly taken concrete form. In the darkness the man's pale forehead stood out, and it was a young forehead, though carved with the wrinkles of long poverty and hardship. His khaki trousers had been slightly pulled up; on his sockless feet he wore a pair of battered gym shoes. She could not see his face and suddenly had an overmastering desire to get one glimpse of it.

She walked to the head of the bench and looked down. The man's head was half buried in his arms, but Toshiko could see that he was surprisingly young. She noticed the thick eyebrows and the fine bridge of his nose. His slightly open mouth was alive with youth.

But Toshiko had approached too close. In the silent night the newspaper bedding rustled, and abruptly the man opened his eyes. Seeing the young woman standing directly beside him, he raised himself with a jerk, and his eyes lit up. A second later a powerful hand reached out and seized Toshiko by her slender wrist.

She did not feel in the least afraid and made no effort to free herself. In a flash the thought had struck her. Ah, so the twenty years have already gone by! The forest of the Imperial Palace was pitch dark and utterly silent.

*Translated by Ivan Morris*

## JAMES THURBER

# If Grant Had Been Drinking at Appomattox

THE MORNING of the ninth of April, 1865, dawned beautifully. General Meade was up with the first streaks of crimson in the eastern sky. General Hooker and General Burnside were up, and had breakfasted, by a quarter after eight. The day continued beautiful. It drew on toward eleven o'clock. General Ulysses S. Grant was still not up. He was asleep in his famous old navy hammock, swung high above the floor of his headquarters' bedroom. Headquarters was distressingly disarranged: papers were strewn on the floor; confidential notes from spies scurried here and there in the breeze from an open window; the dregs of an overturned bottle of wine flowed pinkly across an important military map.

Corporal Shultz, of the Sixty-fifth Ohio Voluntary Infantry, aide to General Grant, came into the outer room, looked around him, and sighed. He entered the bedroom and shook the General's hammock roughly. General Ulysses S. Grant opened one eye.

"Pardon, sir," said Corporal Shultz, "but this is the day of surrender. You ought to be up, sir."

"Don't swing me," said Grant, sharply, for his aide was making the hammock sway gently. "I feel terrible," he added, and he turned over and closed his eye again.

"General Lee will be here any minute now," said the Corporal firmly, swinging the hammock again.

"Will you cut that out?" roared Grant. "D'ya want to make me sick, or what?" Shultz clicked his heels and saluted. "What's he coming here for?" asked the General.

"This is the day of surrender, sir," said Shultz. Grant grunted bitterly.

"Three hundred and fifty generals in the Northern armies," said Grant, "and he has to come to *me* about this. What time is it?"

"You're the Commander-in-Chief, that's why," said Corporal Shultz. "It's eleven twenty-five, sir."

"Don't be crazy," said Grant. "Lincoln is the Commander-in-Chief. Nobody in the history of the world ever surrendered before lunch. Doesn't he know that an army surrenders on its stomach?" He pulled a blanket up over his head and settled himself again.

"The generals of the Confederacy will be here any minute now," said the Corporal. "You really ought to be up, sir."

Grant stretched his arms above his head and yawned.

"All right, all right," he said. He rose to a sitting position and stared about the room. "This place looks awful," he growled.

"You must have had quite a time of it last night, sir," ventured Shultz.

"Yeh," said General Grant, looking around for his clothes. "I was wrassling some general. Some general with a beard."

Shultz helped the commander of the Northern armies in the field to find his clothes.

"Where's my other sock?" demanded Grant. Shultz began to look around for it. The General walked uncertainly to a table and poured a drink from a bottle.

"I don't think it wise to drink, sir," said Shultz.

"Nev' mind about me," said Grant, helping himself to a second, "I can take it or let it alone. Didn' ya ever hear the story about the fella went to Lincoln to complain about me drinking too much? 'So and-So says Grant drinks too much,' this fella said. 'So-and-So is a fool,' said Lincoln. So this fella went to What's-His-Name and told him what Lincoln said and he came roarin' to Lincoln about it. 'Did you tell So-and-So I was a fool?' he said. 'No,' said Lincoln, 'I thought he knew it.' " The General smiled, reminiscently, and had another drink. "*That's* how I stand with Lincoln," he said, proudly.

The soft thudding sound of horses' hooves came through the open window. Shultz hurriedly walked over and looked out.

"Hoof steps," said Grant, with a curious chortle.

"It is General Lee and his staff," said Shultz.

"Show him in," said the General, taking another drink. "And see what the boys in the back room will have."

Shultz walked smartly over to the door, opened it, saluted, and stood aside. General Lee, dignified against the blue of the April sky, magnificent in his dress uniform, stood for a moment framed in the doorway. He walked in, followed by his staff. They bowed, and stood silent. General Grant stared at them. He only had one boot on and his jacket was unbuttoned.

"I know who you are," said Grant. "You're Robert Browning, the poet."

"This is General Robert E. Lee," said one of his staff, coldly.

"Oh," said Grant, "I thought he was Robert Browning. He certainly looks like Robert Browning. There was a poet for you, Lee: Browning. Did ja ever read 'How They Brought the Good News from Ghent to Aix'? 'Up Derek, to saddle, up Derek, away; up Dunder, up Blitzen, up Prancer, up Dancer, up Bouncer, up Vixen, up—' "

"Shall we proceed at once to the matter in hand?" asked General Lee, his eyes disdainfully taking in the disordered room.

"Some of the boys was wrassling here last night,"

explained Grant. "I threw Sherman, or some general a whole lot like Sherman. It was pretty dark." He handed a bottle of Scotch to the commanding officer of the Southern armies, who stood holding it, in amazement and discomfiture. "Get a glass, somebody," said Grant, looking straight at General Longstreet. "Didn't I meet you at Cold Harbor?" he asked. General Longstreet did not answer.

"I should like to have this over with as soon as possible," said Lee. Grant looked vaguely at Shultz, who walked up close to him, frowning.

"The surrender, sir, the surrender," said Corporal Shultz in a whisper.

"Oh sure, sure," said Grant. He took another drink. "All right," he said. "Here we go." Slowly, sadly, he unbuckled his sword. Then he handed it to the astonished Lee. "There you are, General," said Grant. "We dam' near licked you. If I'd been feeling better we *would* of licked you."

## DORIS LESSING

# Homage for Isaac Babel

THE DAY I HAD PROMISED to take Catherine down to visit my young friend Philip at his school in the country, we were to leave at eleven, but she arrived at nine. Her blue dress was new, and so were her fashionable shoes. Her hair had just been done. She looked more than ever like a pink-and-gold Renoir girl who expects everything from life.

Catherine lives in a white house overlooking the sweeping brown tides of the river. She helped me clean up my flat with a devotion which said that she felt small flats were altogether more romantic than large houses. We drank tea, and talked mainly about Philip, who, being fifteen, has pure stern tastes in everything from food to music. Catherine looked at the books lying around his room, and asked if she might borrow the stories of Isaac Babel to read on the train. Catherine is thirteen. I suggested she might find them difficult, but she said: "Philip reads them, doesn't he?"

During the journey I read newspapers and watched her pretty frowning face as she turned the pages of Babel, for she was determined to let nothing get between her and her ambition to be worthy of Philip.

At the school, which is charming, civilized, and expensive, the two children walked together across green fields, and I followed, seeing how the sun gilded their bright friendly heads turned towards each other as they talked. In Catherine's left hand she carried the stories of Isaac Babel.

After lunch we went to the pictures. Philip allowed it to be seen that he thought going to the pictures just for the fun of it was not worthy of intelligent people, but he made the concession, for our sakes. For his sake we chose the more serious of the two films that were showing in the little town. It was about a good priest who helped criminals in New York. His goodness, however, was not enough to prevent one of them from being sent to the gas chamber; and Philip and I waited with Catherine in the dark until she had stopped crying and could face the light of a golden evening.

At the entrance of the cinema the doorman was lying in wait for anyone who had red eyes. Grasping Catherine by her suffering arm, he said bitterly: "Yes, why are you crying? He had to be punished for his crime, didn't he?" Catherine stared at him, incredulous. Philip rescued her by saying with disdain: "Some people don't know right from wrong even when it's *demonstrated* to them." The doorman turned his attention to the next red-eyed emerger from the dark; and we went on together to the station, the children silent because of the cruelty of the world.

Finally Catherine said, her eyes wet again: "I think it's all absolutely beastly, and I can't bear to think about it." And Philip said: "But we've got to think about it, don't you see, because if we don't it'll just go on and *on*, don't you see?"

In the train going back to London I sat beside Catherine. She had the stories open in front of her, but she said: "Philip's awfully lucky. I wish I went to that school. Did you notice that girl who said hullo to him in the garden? They must be great friends. I wish my mother would let me have a dress like that, it's *not* fair."

"I thought it was too old for her."

"Oh, *did* you?"

Soon she bent her head again over the book, but almost at once lifted it to say: "Is he a very famous writer?"

"He's a marvellous writer, brilliant, one of the very best."

"Why?"

"Well, for one thing he's so simple. Look how few words he uses, and how strong his stories are."

"I see. Do you know him? Does he live in London?"

"Oh no, he's dead."

"Oh. Then why did you—I thought he was alive, the way you talked."

"I'm sorry, I suppose I wasn't thinking of him as dead."

"When did he die?"

"He was murdered. About twenty years ago, I suppose."

*"Twenty years."* Her hands began the movement of pushing the book over to me, but then relaxed. "I'll be fourteen in November," she stated, sounding threatened, while her eyes challenged me.

I found it hard to express my need to apologize, but before I could speak, she said, patiently attentive again: "You said he was murdered?"

"Yes."

"I expect the person who murdered him felt sorry when he discovered he had murdered a famous writer."

"Yes, I expect so."

"Was he old when he was murdered?"

"No, quite young really."

"Well, that was bad luck, wasn't it?"

"Yes, I suppose it was bad luck."

"Which do you think is the very best story here? I mean, in your honest opinion, the very very best one."

I chose the story about killing the goose. She read it slowly, while I sat waiting, wishing to take it from her, wishing to protect this charming little person from Isaac Babel.

When she had finished, she said: "Well, some of it I don't understand. He's got a funny way of looking at things. Why should a man's legs in boots look like *girls*?" She finally pushed the book over at me, and said: "I think it's all morbid."

"But you have to understand the kind of life he had. First, he was a Jew in Russia. That was bad enough. Then his experience was all revolution and civil war and. . . ."

But I could see these words bounding off the clear glass of her fiercely denying gaze; and I said: "Look, Catherine, why don't you try again when you're older? Perhaps you'll like him better then?"

She said gratefully: "Yes, perhaps that would be best. After all, Philip is two years older than me, isn't he?"

A week later I got a letter from Catherine.

Thank you very much for being kind enough to take me to visit Philip at his school. It was the most lovely day in my whole life. I am extremely grateful to you for taking me. I have been thinking about the Hoodlum Priest. That was a film which demonstrated to me beyond any shadow of doubt that Capital Punishment is a Wicked Thing, and I shall never forget what I learned that afternoon, and the lessons of it will be with me all my life. I have been meditating about what you said about Isaac Babel, the famed Russian short story writer, and I now see that the conscious simplicity of his style is what makes him, beyond the shadow of a doubt, the great writer that he is, and now in my school compositions I am endeavoring to emulate him so as to learn a conscious simplicity which is the only basis for a really brilliant writing style. Love, Catherine. P.S. Has Philip said anything about my party? I wrote but he hasn't answered. Please find out if he is coming or if he just forgot to answer my letter. I hope he comes, because sometimes I feel I shall die if he doesn't. P.P.S. Please don't tell him I said anything, because I should die if he knew. Love, Catherine.

## JORGE LUIS BORGES

# The Dead Man

THAT A MAN from the suburbs of Buenos Aires, a wistful *compadrito*, with no other virtue than an infatuation with courage, should penetrate the equestrian wastelands along the Brazilian-Argentine frontier and become a captain of contrabandists would seem, initially, impossible. To those who think so, I should like to recount the story of Benjamín Otálora, of whom there is probably not so much as a memory left in the Balvanera quarter, and who died according to his own law, from a bullet, on the borders of Río Grande do Sul. I do not know the details of his adventure; when they are given me, I shall rectify and amplify these pages. For the moment, the following résumé may serve.

In about 1891, Benjamín Otálora is nineteen years old. He is a bully with a low brow, ingenuous light eyes and Basque robustness. A lucky knife thrust has revealed to him that he is brave; the death of his opponent does not disquiet him, nor does the immediate need to flee the Argentine. The boss of his parish gives him a letter for a certain Azevedo Bandeira, of Uruguay. Otálora embarks; the crossing is stormy and the ship works hard; the next day he wanders through the streets of Montevideo with unconfessed and perhaps even unconscious sadness. He does not find Azevedo Bandeira; toward midnight, in a dive on the Paso del Molino, he is a witness to an altercation between a number of cattle drovers. A knife flashes; Otálora does not know which side is in the right but he is attracted by the pure taste of danger, as others are attracted by playing cards or music. In the confusion he fends off a low knife thrust by a *peón* against a man wearing a dark slouch hat and a poncho. This man turns out to be Azevedo Bandeira. (When Otálora finds out, he tears up the letter to him, preferring to owe everything to himself.) Though husky, Azevedo Bandeira gives an unjustified impression of being deformed; in his face, always looming too close, are the Jew, the Negro, and the Indian; in his look, the monkey and the tiger; the scar which cuts across his face is one more ornament, like his black bristly mustache.

The alteraction—a projection or error of alcohol—comes to an end with the same rapidity with which it began. Otálora drinks with the drovers and later accompanies them to a party, and still later to a big house in the Old City, the sun by now high in the sky. In the innermost patio, which is of earth, the men spread out their gear to sleep on. Otálora dimly compares this night with the previous one: now he walks on solid ground, among friends. True, he feels a bit uneasy that he does not miss Buenos Aires. He sleeps until the hour for morning prayer, when he is awakened by the countryman who had drunkenly attacked Bandeira. (Otálora recalls that this man shared with the others the tumultuous and jubilant night and that Bandeira sat him down at his right and obliged him to go on drinking.) The man tells him that the Chief has sent for him. In a kind of office leading into the entranceway (Otálora had never seen an entranceway with lateral doors), Azevedo Bandeira is awaiting him, in the company of a fine disdainful woman with red hair. Bandeira appraises him, offers him a shot of cane brandy, repeats that Otálora strikes him as a brave man, proposes he go north with the rest of them to bring back a herd. Otálora accepts; toward dawn they are on the road, en route to Tacuarembó.

Otálora now begins a different life, a life of vast dawns and of days smelling of horses. It is a new life for him, sometimes an atrocious one, but it has already passed into his bloodstream, for just as men of other nations venerate and feel a presentiment of the sea, in the same way we Argentines (including the man who interweaves these symbols) long for the inexhaustible plains which resound beneath the hooves. Otálora was raised in the quarter of the city inhabited by carters and wagoners; before a year is out, he has become a gaucho. He learns to ride, to round up the cattle on the hacienda, to slaughter on the range, to handle the lasso and the bolas that fell cattle, to fight off sleep, to endure storms and frost and sun, to drive livestock with whistles and cries. Only once in all this time of apprenticeship does he see Azevedo Bandeira, but the latter is very much in his mind, for to be *one of Bandeira's men* is to be highly considered and feared, and because, in the face of any and all manliness, the gauchos say "Bandeira does it better." Someone asserts that Bandeira was born on the other side of the Cuareim, in Río Grande do Sul: this attribution, which should make him less, adds a dimension and mysteriously leagues him with thick jungles, with swamps, with inextricable and almost infinite distances. Gradually, Otálora realizes that Bandeira's affairs are multiple and that chief among them is smuggling. To be a cattle drover is to be a serf; Otálora determines to rise to the rank of contrabandist. One night, two comrades are to cross the frontier and bring back a quantity of cane brandy; Otálora picks a quarrel with one of them, wounds him, and then takes his place. He is moved to it by ambition, and also by some dark sense of loyalty. *Let that man* (he thinks) *realize, once and for all, that I'm worth more than all his Uruguayans put together.*

A year passes before Otálora returns to Montevideo. The party rides along the river bank, around the city (which strikes Otálora as immense); they arrive at the Chief's house; the men spread out their gear in the inmost patio. The days pass and

Otálora still has not seen Bandeira. They say, fearfully, that he is sick; a mulatto customarily takes up his soup caldron and his maté tea to his quarters. One afternoon, Otálora is entrusted with the job. He feels a vague humiliation, but also satisfaction.

The bedroom is dilapidated and dark. There is a balcony facing west, a long table covered with whips, horsewhips, gun and cartridge belts, firearms and knives, and there is a remote mirror with its glass dimmed. Bandeira lies face upward; he dreams and moans; the vehemence of a final sun outlines him. The vast white bed seems to diminish and obscure him; Otálora takes note of the gray hair, the fatigue, the flaccidity, the fissures of the years. He is revolted at the thought that this old man should be their leader. It occurs to him that a single blow would be enough to take care of the man in the bed. At this juncture he notices in the mirror that someone has come into the room. It is the red-haired woman; she is half-dressed and barefoot, and she observes him with cold curiosity. Bandeira sits up; while he talks of country matters and drinks one maté after another, his fingers play with the woman's braids. At last, he gives Otálora permission to withdraw.

Days later, the order to go north is given. They ride to a lost far-off country house, which stands as it might have stood in any other part whatsoever of the interminable plain. Neither trees nor a stream gladden it; the first sun and the last beat upon it. The hacienda boasts stone corrals, but the whole place is run down. This poor place is called *The Sigh*.

Otálora learns, from a discussion among the *peones*, that Bandeira will soon be coming from Montevideo. He asks why, and is told that there is an outsider among them, an outsider-turned-gaucho who is trying to take over. Otálora realizes that they are joking, but he is flattered that such a joke has become possible. He learns, a bit later, that

Bandeira has fallen out with one of the political chieftains and that the latter has withdrawn his support. This news pleases him.

Boxes of long weapons begin to arrive; a silver jar and basin arrive for the woman's quarters; intricate damask curtains arrive; out of the mountain range, one morning, rides a somber horseman, with a heavy beard and wearing a poncho. His name is Ulpiano Suárez, and he is Azevedo Bandiera's *capanga* or bodyguard. He says little and speaks with Brazilian intonations. Otálora does not know whether to attribute his reserve to hostility, scorn, or mere barbarity. He does know, for sure, that in order to carry out the plan he is hatching, he must gain his favor.

A reddish horse with black points next enters into Benjamín Otálora's destiny; it is brought from the South by Azevedo Bandeira, and it boasts accouterments covered with metal and saddle padding bordered with tiger skin. This free-spirited horse is a symbol of the Chief's authority, and for that reason the boy covets it; he also desires, with a rancorous desire, the woman with the luminous hair. The woman, the accouterments, and the reddish horse are attributes or adjectives of a man whom he aspires to destroy.

Here the story becomes complicated, more profound. Azevedo Bandeíra is an expert in the art of progressive intimidation, in the satanic maneuver of gradually humiliating his interlocutor by combining verities and gibes; Otálora resolves to apply this ambiguous method to the hard task he has set himself. He resolves to supplant, slowly, Azevedo Bandeira. He gains, during days of common danger, the friendship of Suárez. He confides in him his plan; Suárez promises his help. Many things happen thereafter, a small number of which I know about. Otálora does not carry out Bandeira's orders: he overlooks them, corrects them, invents them. The entire universe seems to conspire along with him, and to hasten events. One noonday, in some fields in Tacuarembó, there is an exchange of gunfire with a gang from Río Grande province; Otálora usurps Bandeira's place and takes command of the Uruguayans. A bullet goes through his shoulder, but that afternoon Otálora rides back to *The Sigh* on the red horse of the Chief, and that afternoon some drops of his blood stain the tiger skin, and that night he sleeps with the woman with the luminous hair. Other versions of the story change the order of these events and even deny that they all occurred in one day.

Bandeira, nevertheless, is always nominally Chief. He issues orders which are not executed. Benjamín Otálora does not touch him, for mixed reasons of custom and pity.

The last scene of the drama corresponds to the upheaval of the last night. That night, the men at *The Sigh* eat freshly slaughtered meat, and drink a fighting liquor; someone infinitely draws out flourishes of an elaborate *milonga* on the guitar. At the head of the table, Otálora, drunk, adds exultation to exultation, jubilation to jubilation; this vertiginous tower becomes a symbol of his irresistible destiny. Bandeira, taciturn among the shouters, lets the night flow clamorously along. When the bell tolls twelve, he rises like a man remembering an obligation. He gets up and knocks softly at the woman's door. She opens to him swiftly, as if she had been awaiting his call. She comes out half-dressed and barefoot. In a voice grown effeminate, a voice which comes thickly, the Chief gives an order:

"Now that you and the man from Buenos Aires are so much in love, you can go and give him a kiss right in front of everybody."

He adds a brutal particular, an obscene detail. The woman tries to resist, but two men take her by the arm and push her upon Otálora. Dissolving in tears, she kisses his face and chest. Ulpiano Suárez has taken his revolver in his hand. Otálora realizes before he dies, that they have betrayed him from the start, that he has been condemned to death;

that they have allowed him to make love, to command, to triumph, because they had already given him up for dead, because in Bandeira's eyes he was already dead.

Suárez, almost scornfully, pulls the trigger.

*Translated by Anthony Kerrigan*

## VARLAM SHALAMOV

# In the Night

SUPPER WAS OVER. Slowly Glebov licked the bowl and brushed the bread crumbs methodically from the table into his left palm. Without swallowing, he felt each miniature fragment of bread in his mouth coated greedily with a thick layer of saliva. Glebov couldn't have said whether it tasted good or not. Taste was an entirely different thing, not worthy to be compared with this passionate sensation that made all else recede into oblivion. Glebov was in no hurry to swallow; the bread itself melted in his mouth and quickly vanished.

Bagretsov's cavernous, gleaming eyes stared into Glebov's mouth without interruption. None of them had enough will power to take his eyes from food disappearing in another's mouth. Glebov swallowed his saliva, and Bagretsov immediately shifted his gaze to the horizon—to the large orange moon crawling out onto the sky.

"It's time," said Bagretsov. Slowly they set out along a path leading to a large rock and climbed up onto a small terrace encircling the hill. Although the sun had just set, cold had already settled into the rocks that in the daytime burned the soles of feet that were bare inside the rubber galoshes. Glebov buttoned his quilted jacket. Walking provided no warmth.

"Is it much farther?" he asked in a whisper.

"Some way," Bagretsov answered quietly.

They sat down to rest. They had nothing to say

or even think of—everything was clear and simple. In a flat area at the end of the terrace were mounds of stone dug from the ground and drying moss that had been ripped from its bed.

"I could have handled this myself," Bagretsov smiled wryly. "But it's more cheerful work if there are two of us. Then, too I figured you were an old friend. . . ."

They had both been brought on the same ship the previous year.

Bagretsov stopped: "Get down or they'll see us."

They lay down and began to toss the stones to the side. None of the rocks was too big for two men to lift since the people who had heaped them up that morning were no stronger than Glebov.

Bagretsov swore quietly. He had cut his finger and the blood was flowing. He sprinkled sand on the wound, ripped a piece of wadding from his jacket, and pressed it against the cut, but the blood wouldn't stop.

"Poor coagulation," Glebov said indifferently.

"Are you a doctor?" asked Bagretsov, sucking the wound.

Glebov remained silent. The time when he had been a doctor seemed very far away. Had it ever existed? Too often the world beyond the mountains and seas seemed unreal, like something out of a dream. Real were the minute, the hour, the day—from reveille to the end of work. He never guessed further, nor did he have the strength to guess. Nor did anyone else.

He didn't know the past of the people who surrounded him and didn't want to know. But then, if tomorrow Bagretsov were to declare himself a doctor of philosophy or a marshal of aviation, Glebov would believe him without a second thought. Had he himself really been a doctor? Not only the habit of judgment was lost, but even the habit of observation. Glebov watched Bagretsov suck the blood from his finger but said nothing. The circumstance slid across his consciousness, but he couldn't find or even seek within himself the will to answer. The consciousness that remained to him—the consciousness that was perhaps no longer human—had too few facets and was now directed toward one goal only, that of removing the stones as quickly as possible.

"Is it deep?" Glebov asked when they stopped to rest.

"How can it be deep?" Bagretsov replied.

And Glebov realized his question was absurd, that of course the hole couldn't be deep.

"Here he is," Bagretsov said. He reached out to touch a human toe. The big toe peered out from under the rocks and was perfectly visible in the moonlight. The toe was different from Glebov's and Bagretsov's toes—but not in that it was lifeless and stiff; there was very little difference in this regard. The nail of the dead toe was clipped, and the toe itself was fuller and softer than Glebov's. They quickly tossed aside the remaining stones heaped over the body.

"He's a young one," Bagretsov said.

Together the two of them dragged the corpse from the grave.

"He's so big and healthy," Glebov said, panting.

"If he weren't so fattened up," Bagretsov said, "they would have buried him the way they bury us, and there would have been no reason for us to come here today."

They straightened out the corpse and pulled off the shirt.

"You know, the shorts are like new," Bagretsov said with satisfaction.

Glebov hid the underwear under his jacket.

"Better to wear it," Bagretsov said.

"No, I don't want to," Glebov muttered.

They put the corpse back in the grave and heaped it over with rocks.

The blue light of the rising moon fell on the rocks and the scant forest of the taiga, revealing each projecting rock, each tree in a peculiar fashion, different from the way they looked by day. Everything seemed real but different than in the daytime. It was as if the world had a second face, a nocturnal face.

The dead man's underwear was warm under Glebov's jacket and no longer seemed alien.

"I need a smoke," Glebov said in a dreamlike fashion.

"Tomorrow you'll get your smoke."

Bagretsov smiled. Tomorrow they would sell the underwear, trade it for bread, maybe even get some tobacco. . . .

*Translated by John Glad*

OCTAVIO PAZ

# The Blue Bouquet

I WOKE COVERED WITH SWEAT. Hot steam rose from the newly sprayed, red-brick pavement. A gray-winged butterfly, dazzled, circled the yellow light. I jumped from my hammock and crossed the room barefoot, careful not to step on some scorpion leaving his hideout for a bit of fresh air. I went to the little window and inhaled the country air. One could hear the breathing of the night, feminine, enormous. I returned to the center of the room, emptied water from a jar into a pewter basin, and wet my towel. I rubbed my chest and legs with the soaked cloth, dried myself a little, and, making sure that no bugs were hidden in the folds of my clothes, got dressed. I ran down the green stairway. At the door of the boardinghouse I bumped into the owner, a one-eyed taciturn fellow. Sitting on a wicker stool, he smoked, his eye half closed. In a hoarse voice, he asked:

"Where are you going?"

"To take a walk. It's too hot."

"Hmmm—everything's closed. And no streetlights around here. You'd better stay put."

I shrugged my shoulders, muttered "back soon," and plunged into the darkness. At first I couldn't see anything. I fumbled along the cobblestone street. I lit a cigarette. Suddenly the moon appeared from behind a black cloud, lighting a white wall that was crumbled in places. I stopped, blinded by such whiteness. Wind whistled slightly. I breathed the air of the tamarinds. The night hummed, full of leaves and insects. Crickets bivouacked in the tall grass. I raised my head: up there the stars too had set up camp. I thought that the universe was a vast system of signs, a conversation between giant beings. My actions, the cricket's saw, the star's blink, were nothing but pauses and syllables, scattered phrases from that dialogue. What word could it be, of which I was only a syllable? Who speaks the word? To whom is it spoken? I threw my cigarette down on the sidewalk. Falling, it drew a shining curve, shooting out brief sparks like a tiny comet.

I walked a long time, slowly. I felt free, secure between the lips that were at that moment speaking me with such happiness. The night was a garden of eyes. As I crossed the street, I heard someone come out of a doorway. I turned around, but could not distinguish anything. I hurried on. A few moments later I heard the dull shuffle of sandals on the hot stone. I didn't want to turn around, although I felt the shadow getting closer with every step. I tried to run. I couldn't. Suddenly I stopped short. Before I could defend myself, I felt the point of a knife in my back, and a sweet voice:

"Don't move, mister, or I'll stick it in."

Without turning, I asked:

"What do you want?"

"Your eyes, mister," answered the soft, almost painful voice.

"My eyes? What do you want with my eyes? Look, I've got some money. Not much, but it's something. I'll give you everything I have if you let me go. Don't kill me."

"Don't be afraid, mister. I won't kill you. I'm only going to take your eyes."

"But why do you want my eyes?" I asked again.

"My girlfriend has this whim. She wants a bouquet of blue eyes. And around here they're hard to find."

"My eyes won't help you. They're brown, not blue."

"Don't try to fool me, mister. I know very well that yours are blue."

"Don't take the eyes of a fellow man. I'll give you something else."

"Don't play saint with me," he said harshly. "Turn around."

I turned. He was small and fragile. His palm sombrero covered half his face. In his right hand he held a country machete that shone in the moonlight.

"Let me see your face."

I struck a match and put it close to my face. The brightness made me squint. He opened my eyelids with a firm hand. He couldn't see very well. Standing on tiptoe, he stared at me intensely. The flame burned my fingers. I dropped it. A silent moment passed.

"Are you convinced now? They're not blue."

"Pretty clever, aren't you?" he answered. "Let's see. Light another one."

I struck another match, and put it near my eyes. Grabbing my sleeve, he ordered:

"Kneel down."

I knelt. With one hand he grabbed me by the hair, pulling my head back. He bent over me, curious and tense, while his matchete slowly dropped until it grazed my eyelids. I closed my eyes.

"Keep them open," he ordered.

I opened my eyes. The flame burned my lashes. All of a sudden he let me go.

"All right, they're not blue. Beat it."

He vanished. I leaned against the wall, my head in my hands. I pulled myself together. Stumbling, falling, trying to get up again. I ran for an hour through the deserted town. When I got to the plaza, I saw the owner of the boardinghouse, still sitting in the front of the door. I went in without saying a word. The next day I left town.

JEROME WEIDMAN

# My Father Sits in the Dark

MY FATHER has a peculiar habit. He is fond of sitting in the dark, alone. Sometimes I come home very late. The house is dark. I let myself in quietly because I do not want to disturb my mother. She is a light sleeper. I tiptoe into my room and undress in the dark. I go to the kitchen for a drink of water. My bare feet make no noise. I step into the room and almost trip over my father. He is sitting in a kitchen chair, in his pajamas, smoking his pipe.

"Hello, Pop," I say.

"Hello, son."

"Why don't you go to bed, Pa?"

"I will," he says.

But he remains there. Long after I am asleep I feel sure that he is still sitting there, smoking.

Many times I am reading in my room. I hear my mother get the house ready for the night. I hear my kid brother go to bed. I hear my sister come in. I hear her do things with jars and combs until she, too, is quiet. I know she has gone to sleep. In a little while I hear my mother say good night to my father. I continue to read. Soon I become thirsty. (I drink a lot of water.) I go to the kitchen for a drink. Again I almost stumble across my father. Many times it startles me. I forget about him. And there he is—smoking, sitting, thinking.

"Why don't you go to bed, Pop?"

"I will, son."

But he doesn't. He just sits there and smokes and

thinks. It worries me. I can't understand it. What can he be thinking about? Once I asked him.

"What are you thinking about, Pa?"

"Nothing," he said.

Once I left him there and went to bed. I awoke several hours later. I was thirsty. I went to the kitchen. There he was. His pipe was out. But he sat there, staring into a corner of the kitchen. After a moment I became accustomed to the darkness. I took my drink. He still sat and stared. His eyes did not blink. I thought he was not even aware of me. I was afraid.

"Why don't you go to bed, Pop?"

"I will, son," he said. "Don't wait up for me."

"But," I said, "you've been sitting here for hours. What's wrong? What are you thinking about?"

"Nothing, son," he said. "Nothing. It's just restful. That's all."

The way he said it was convincing. He did not seem worried. His voice was even and pleasant. It always is. But I could not understand it. How could it be restful to sit alone in an uncomfortable chair far into the night, in darkness?

What can it be?

I review all the possibilities. It can't be money. I know that. We haven't much, but when he is worried about money he makes no secret of it. It can't be his health. He is not reticent about that either. It can't be the health of anyone in the family. We are a bit short on money, but we are long on health. (Knock wood, my mother would say.) What can it be? I am afraid I do not know. But that does not stop me from worrying.

Maybe he is thinking of his brothers in the old country. Or of his mother and two step-mothers. Or of his father. But they are all dead. And he would not brood about them like that. I say brood, but it is not really true. He does not brood. He does not even seem to be thinking. He looks too peaceful, too, well not contented, just too peaceful, to be brooding.

Perhaps it is as he says. Perhaps it is restful. But it does not seem possible. It worries me.

If I only knew what he thinks about. If I only knew that he thinks at all. I might not be able to help him. He might not even need help. It may be as he says. It may be restful. But at least I would not worry about it.

Why does he just sit there, in the dark? Is his mind failing? No, it can't be. He is only fifty-three. And he is just as keen-witted as ever. In fact, he is the same in every respect. He still likes beet soup. He still reads the second section of the *Times* first. He still wears wing collars. He still believes that Debs could have saved the country and that T.R. was a tool of the moneyed interests. He is the same in every way. He does not even look older than he did five years ago. Everybody remarks about that. Well-preserved, they say. But he sits in the dark, alone, smoking, staring straight ahead of him, unblinking, into the small hours of the night.

If it is as he says, if it is restful, I will let it go at that. But suppose it is not. Suppose it is something I cannot fathom. Perhaps he needs help. Why doesn't he speak? Why doesn't he frown or laugh or cry? Why doesn't he do something? Why does he just sit there?

Finally I become angry. Maybe it is just my unsatisfied curiosity. Maybe I *am* a bit worried. Anyway, I become angry.

"Is something wrong, Pop?"

"Nothing, son. Nothing at all."

But this time I am determined not to be put off. I am angry.

"Then why do you sit here all alone, thinking, till late?"

"It's restful, son. I like it."

I am getting nowhere. Tomorrow he will be sitting there again. I will be puzzled. I will be worried. I will not stop now. I am angry.

"Well, what do you *think* about, Pa? Why do you just sit here? What's worrying you? What do you think about?"

"Nothing's worrying me, son. I'm all right. It's just restful. That's all. Go to bed, son."

My anger has left me. But the feeling of worry is still there. I must get an answer. It seems so silly. Why doesn't he tell me? I have a funny feeling that unless I get an answer I will go crazy. I am insistent.

"But what do you *think* about, Pa? What is it?"

"Nothing, son. Just things in general. Nothing special. Just things."

I can get no answer.

It is very late. The street is quiet and the house is dark. I climb the steps softly, skipping the ones that creak. I let myself in with my key and tiptoe into my room. I remove my clothes and remember that I am thirsty. In my bare feet I walk to the kitchen. Before I reach it I know he is there.

I can see the deeper darkness of his hunched shape. He is sitting in the same chair, his elbows on his knees, his cold pipe in his teeth, his unblinking eyes staring straight ahead. He does not seem to know I am there. He did not hear me come in. I stand quietly in the doorway and watch him.

Everything is quiet, but the night is full of little sounds. As I stand there motionless I begin to notice them. The ticking of the alarm clock on the icebox. The low hum of an automobile passing many blocks away. The swish of papers moved along the street by the breeze. A whispering rise and fall of sound, like low breathing. It is strangely pleasant.

The dryness in my throat reminds me. I step briskly into the kitchen.

"Hello, Pop," I say.

"Hello, son," he says. His voice is low and dreamlike. He does not change his position or shift his gaze.

I cannot find the faucet. The dim shadow of light that comes through the window from the street lamp only makes the room seem darker. I reach for the short chain in the center of the room. I snap on the light.

He straightens up with a jerk, as though he has been struck. "What's the matter, Pop?" I ask.

"Nothing," he says. "I don't like the light."

"What's the matter with the light?" I say. "What's wrong?"

"Nothing," he says. "I don't like the light."

I snap the light off. I drink my water slowly. I must take it easy, I say to myself. I must get to the bottom of this.

"Why don't you go to bed? Why do you sit here so late in the dark?"

"It's nice, he says. "I can't get used to lights. We didn't have lights when I was a boy in Europe."

My heart skips a beat and I catch my breath happily. I begin to think I understand. I remember the stories of his boyhood in Austria. I see the wide-beamed *kretchma,* with my grandfather behind the bar. It is late, the customers are gone, and he is dozing. I see the bed of glowing coals, the last of the roaring fire. The room is already dark, and grower darker. I see a small boy, crouched on a pile of twigs at one side of the huge fireplace, his starry gaze fixed on the dull remains of the dead flames. The boy is my father.

I remember the pleasure of those few moments while I stood quietly in the doorway watching him.

"You mean there's nothing wrong? You just sit in the dark because you like it, Pop?" I find it hard to keep my voice from rising in a happy shout.

"Sure," he says. "I can't think with the light on."

I set my glass down and turn to go back to my room. "Good night, Pop," I say.

"Good night," he says.

Then I remember. I turn back. "What do you think about, Pop?" I ask.

His voice seems to come from far away. It is quiet and even again. "Nothing," he says softly. "Nothing special."

## GRACE PALEY

# Wants

I SAW MY EX-HUSBAND in the street. I was sitting on the steps of the new library.

Hello, my life, I said. We had once been married for twenty-seven years, so I felt justified.

He said, What? What life? No life of mine.

I said, O.K. I don't argue when there's real disagreement. I got up and went into the library to see how much I owed them.

The librarian said $32 even and you've owed it for eighteen years. I didn't deny anything. Because I don't understand how time passes. I have had those books. I have often thought of them. The library is only two blocks away.

My ex-husband followed me to the Books Returned desk. He interrupted the librarian, who had more to tell. In many ways, he said, as I look back, I attribute the dissolution of our marriage to the fact that you never invited the Bertrams to dinner.

That's possible, I said. But really, if you remember: first, my father was sick that Friday, then the children were born, then I had those Tuesday-night meetings, then the war began. Then we didn't seem to know them any more. But you're right. I should have had them to dinner.

I gave the librarian a check for $32. Immediately she trusted me, put my past behind her, wiped the record clean, which is just what most other municipal and/or state bureaucracies will *not* do.

I checked out the two Edith Wharton books I had

just returned because I'd read them so long ago and they are more apropos now than ever. They were *The House of Mirth* and *The Children,* which is about how life in the United States in New York changed in twenty-seven years fifty years ago.

A nice thing I do remember is breakfast, my ex-husband said. I was surprised. All we ever had was coffee. Then I remembered there was a hole in the back of the kitchen closet which opened into the apartment next door. There, they always ate sugar-cured smoked bacon. It gave us a very grand feeling about breakfast, but we never got stuffed and sluggish.

That was when we were poor, I said.

When were we ever rich? he asked.

Oh, as time went on, as our responsibilities increased, we didn't go in need. You took adequate financial care, I reminded him. The children went to camp four weeks a year and in decent ponchos with sleeping bags and boots, just like everyone else. They looked very nice. Our place was warm in winter, and we had nice red pillows and things.

I wanted a sailboat, he said. But you didn't want anything.

Don't be bitter, I said. It's never too late.

No, he said with a great deal of bitterness. I may get a sailboat. As a matter of fact I have money down on an eighteen-foot two-rigger. I'm doing well this year and can look forward to better. But as for you, it's too late. You'll always want nothing.

He had had a habit throughout the twenty-seven years of making a narrow remark which, like a plumber's snake, could work its way through the ear down the throat, halfway to my heart. He would then disappear, leaving me choking with equipment. What I mean is, I sat down on the library steps and he went away.

I looked through *The House of Mirth,* but lost interest. I felt extremely accused. Now, it's true, I'm short of requests and absolute requirements. But I do want *something.*

I want, for instance, to be a different person. I want to be the woman who brings these two books back in two weeks. I want to be the effective citizen who changes the school system and addresses the Board of Estimate on the troubles of this dear urban center.

I *had* promised my children to end the war before they grew up.

I wanted to have been married forever to one person, my ex-husband or my present one. Either has enough character for a whole life, which as it turns out is really not such a long time. You couldn't exhaust either man's qualities or get under the rock of his reasons in one short life.

Just this morning I looked out the window to watch the street for a while and saw that the little sycamores the city had dreamily planted a couple of years before the kids were born had come that day to the prime of their lives.

Well! I decided to bring those two books back to the library. Which proves that when a person or an event comes along to jolt or appraise me I *can* take some appropriate action, although I am better known for my hospitable remarks.

## GABRIEL GARCÍA MÁRQUEZ

# Bitterness for Three Sleepwalkers

NOW WE HAD HER THERE, abandoned in a corner of the house. Someone had told us, before we brought her things—her clothes which smelled of newly cut wood, her weightless shoes for the mud—that she would be unable to get used to that slow life, with no sweet tastes, no attraction except that harsh, wattled solitude, always pressing on her back. Someone told us—and a lot of time had passed before we remembered it—that she had also had a childhood. Maybe we didn't believe it then. But now, seeing her sitting in the corner with her frightened eyes and a finger placed on her lips, maybe we accepted the fact that she'd had a childhood, once, that once she'd had a touch that was sensitive to the anticipatory coolness of the rain, and that she always carried an unexpected shadow in profile to her body.

All this—and much more—we believed that afternoon when we realized that above her fearsome subworld she was completely human. We found it out suddenly, as if a glass had been broken inside, when she began to give off anguished shouts; she began to call each one of us by name, speaking amidst tears until we sat down beside her; we began to sing and clap hands as if our shouting could put the scattered pieces of glass back together. Only then were we able to believe that at one time she had had a childhood. It was as if her shouts were like a revelation somehow; as if they had a lot of remembered tree and deep river about them. When she got up, she leaned over a little and, still without covering her face with her apron, still without blowing her nose, and still with tears, she told us:

"I'll never smile again."

We went out into the courtyard, the three of us, not talking; maybe we thought we carried common thoughts. Maybe we thought it would be best not to turn on the lights in the house. She wanted to be alone—maybe—sitting in the dark corner, weaving the final braid which seemed to be the only thing that would survive her passage toward the beast.

Outside, in the courtyard, sunk in the deep vapor of the insects, we sat down to think about her. We'd done it so many times before. We might have said that we were doing what we'd been doing every day of our lives.

Yet it was different that night: she'd said that she would never smile again, and we, who knew her so well, were certain that the nightmare had become the truth. Sitting in a triangle, we imagined her there inside, abstract, incapacitated, unable even to hear the innumerable clocks that measured the marked and minute rhythm with which she was changing into dust. "If we only had the courage at least to wish for her death," we thought in a chorus. But we wanted her like that: ugly and glacial, like a mean contribution to our hidden defects.

We'd been adults since before, since a long time back. She, however, was the oldest in the house. That same night she had been able to be there, sitting with us, feeling the measured throbbing of the stars, surrounded by healthy sons. She would have been the respectable lady of the house if she had been the wife of a solid citizen or the concubine of a punctual man. But she became accustomed to living in only one dimension, like a straight line, perhaps because her vices or her virtues could not be seen in profile. We'd known that for many years now. We weren't even surprised one morning, after getting up, when we found her face down in the courtyard, biting the earth in a hard, ecstatic way. Then she smiled, looked at us again; she had fallen out of the second-story window onto the hard clay of the courtyard and had remained there, stiff and concrete, face down on the damp clay. But later we learned that the only thing she had kept intact was her fear of distances, a natural fright upon facing space. We lifted her up by the shoulders. She wasn't as hard as she had seemed to us at first. On the contrary, her organs were loose, detached from her will, like a lukewarm corpse that hadn't begun to stiffen.

Her eyes were open, her mouth was dirty with that earth that already must have had a taste of sepulchral sediment for her when we turned her face up to the sun, and it was as if we had placed her in front of a mirror. She looked at us all with a dull, sexless expression that gave us—holding her in my arms now—the measure of her absence. Someone told us she was dead; and afterward she remained smiling with that cold and quiet smile that she wore at night when she moved about the house awake. She said she didn't know how she got to the courtyard. She said that she'd felt quite warm, that she'd been listening to a cricket, penetrating, sharp, which seemed—so she said—about to knock down the wall of her room, and that she had set herself to remembering Sunday's prayers, with her cheek tight against the cement floor.

We knew, however, that she couldn't remember any prayer, for we discovered later that she'd lost the notion of time when she said she'd fallen asleep holding up the inside of the wall that the cricket was pushing on from outside and that she was fast asleep when someone, taking her by the shoulders, moved the wall aside and laid her down with her face to the sun.

That night we knew, sitting in the courtyard, that she would never smile again. Perhaps her inexpressive seriousness pained us in anticipation, her dark and willful living in a corner. It pained us deeply, as we were pained the day we saw her sit down in the corner where she was now; and we heard her say that she wasn't going to wander through the house any more. At first we couldn't believe her. We'd seen her for months on end going through the rooms at all hours, her head hard and her shoulders drooping, never stopping, never growing tired. At night we would hear her thick body noise moving between two darknesses, and we would lie awake in bed many times hearing her stealthy walking, following her all through the house with our ears. Once she told us that she had seen the cricket inside the mirror glass, sunken, submerged in the solid transparency, and that it had crossed through the glass surface to reach her. We really didn't know what she was trying to tell us, but we could all see that her clothes were wet, sticking to her body, as if she had just come out of a cistern. Without trying to explain the phenomenon, we decided to do away with the insects in the house: destroy the objects that obsessed her.

We had the walls cleaned; we ordered them to chop down the plants in the courtyard and it was as if we had cleansed the silence of the night of bits of trash. But we no longer heard her walking, nor did we hear her talk about crickets any more, until the day when, after the last meal, she remained looking at us, she sat down on the cement floor, still looking at us, and said: "I'm going to stay here, sitting down," and we shuddered, because we could see that she had begun to look like something already almost completely like death.

That had been a long time ago and we had even grown used to seeing her there, sitting, her braid always half wound, as if she had become dissolved in her solitude and, even though she was there to be seen, had lost her natural faculty of being present. That's why we now knew that she would never smile again; because she had said so in the same convinced and certain way in which she had told us once that she would never walk again. It was as if we were certain that she would tell us later: "I'll never see again," or maybe "I'll never hear again," and we knew that she was sufficiently human to go along willing the elimination of her vital functions and that spontaneously she would go about ending herself, sense by sense, until one day we would find her leaning against the wall, as if she had fallen asleep for the first time in her life. Perhaps there was still a lot of time left for that, but the three of us, sitting in the courtyard, would have liked to hear her sharp and sudden broken-glass weeping that night, at least to give us the illusion that a baby . . . a girl baby had been born in the house. In order to believe that she had been born renewed.

*Translated by Gregory Rabassa*

## AUGUSTO MONTERROSO

# The Eclipse

WHEN BROTHER Bartolome Arrazola felt lost he accepted that nothing could save him anymore. The powerful Guatemalan jungle had trapped him inexorably and definitively. Before his topographical ignorance he sat quietly awaiting death. He wanted to die there, hopelessly and alone, with his thoughts fixed on far-away Spain, particularly on the Los Abrojos convent where Charles the Fifth had once condescended to lessen his prominence and tell him that he trusted the religious zeal of his redemptive work.

Upon awakening he found himself surrounded by a group of indifferent natives who were getting ready to sacrifice him in front of an altar, an altar that to Bartolome seemed to be the place in which he would finally rest from his fears, his destiny, from himself.

Three years in the land had given him a fair knowledge of the native tongues. He tried something. He said a few words which were understood.

He then had an idea he considered worthy of his talent, universal culture and steep knowledge of Aristotle. He remembered that a total eclipse of the sun was expected on that day and in his innermost thoughts he decided to use that knowledge to deceive his oppressors and save his life.

"If you kill me"—he told them, "I can darken the sun in its heights."

The natives looked at him fixedly and Bartolome caught the incredulity in their eyes. He saw that a small counsel was set up and waited confidently, not without some disdain.

Two hours later Brother Bartolome Arrazola's heart spilled its fiery blood on the sacrificial stone (brilliant under the opaque light of an eclipsed sun), while one of the natives recited without raising his voice, unhurriedly, one by one, the infinite dates in which there would be solar and lunar eclipses, that the astronomers of the Mayan community had foreseen and written on their codices without Aristotle's valuable help.

*Translated by Wilfrido H. Corral*

## HEINRICH BÖLL

# The Laugher

WHEN SOMEONE ASKS ME what business I am in, I am seized with embarrassment: I blush and stammer, I who am otherwise known as a man of poise. I envy people who can say: I am a bricklayer. I envy barbers, bookkeepers and writers the simplicity of their avowal, for all these professions speak for themselves and need no lengthy explanation, while I am constrained to reply to such questions: I am a laugher. An admission of this kind demands another, since I have to answer the second question: "Is that how you make your living?" truthfully with "Yes." I actually do make a living at my laughing, and a good one too, for my laughing is—commercially speaking—much in demand. I am a good laugher, experienced, no one else laughs as well as I do, no one else has such command of the fine points of my art. For a long time, in order to avoid tiresome explanations, I called myself an actor, but my talents in the field of mime and elocution are so meager that I felt this designation to be too far from the truth: I love the truth, and the truth is: I am a laugher. I am neither a clown nor a comedian. I do not make people gay, I portray gaiety: I laugh like a Roman emperor, or like a sensitive schoolboy, I am as much at home in the laughter of the seventeenth century as in that of the nineteenth, and when occasion demands I laugh my way through all the centuries, all classes of society, all categories of age: it is simply a skill which I have acquired, like the skill of being able to repair shoes. In my breast I harbor the laughter of America, the laughter of Africa, white, red, yellow laughter—and for the right fee I let it peal out in accordance with the director's requirements.

I have become indispensable; I laugh on records, I laugh on tape, and television directors treat me with respect. I laugh mournfully, moderately, hysterically; I laugh like a streetcar conductor or like a helper in the grocery business; laughter in the morning, laughter in the evening, nocturnal laughter and the laughter of twilight. In short: wherever and however laughter is required—I do it.

It need hardly be pointed out that a profession of this kind is tiring, especially as I have also—this is my specialty—mastered the art of infectious laughter; this has also made me indispensable to third- and fourth-rate comedians, who are scared—and with good reason—that their audiences will miss their punch lines, so I spend most evenings in night clubs as a kind of discreet claque, my job being to laugh infectiously during the weaker parts of the program. It has to be carefully timed: my hearty, boisterous laughter must not come too soon, but neither must it come too late, it must come just at the right spot: at the pre-arranged moment I burst out laughing, the whole audience roars with me, and the joke is saved.

But as for me, I drag myself exhausted to the checkroom, put on my overcoat, happy that I can go off duty at last. At home I usually find telegrams waiting for me: "Urgently require your laughter. Recording Tuesday," and a few hours later I am sitting in an overheated express train bemoaning my fate.

I need scarcely say that when I am off duty or on vacation I have little inclination to laugh: the cowhand is glad when he can forget the cow, the bricklayer when he can forget the mortar, and carpenters usually have doors at home which don't work or drawers which are hard to open. Confectioners like sour pickles, butchers like marzipan, and the baker prefers sausage to bread; bullfighters raise pigeons for a hobby, boxers turn pale when their children have nose-bleeds: I find all this quite natural, for I never laugh off duty. I am a very solemn person, and people consider me—perhaps rightly so—a pessimist.

During the first years of our married life, my wife would often say to me: "Do laugh!" but since then she has come to realize that I cannot grant her this wish. I am happy when I am free to relax my tense face muscles, my frayed spirit, in profound solemnity. Indeed, even other people's laughter gets on my nerves, since it reminds me too much of my profession. So our marriage is a quiet, peaceful one, because my wife has also forgotten how to laugh: now and again I catch her smiling, and I smile too. We converse in low tones, for I detest the noise of the night clubs, the noise that sometimes fills the recording studios. People who do not know me think I am taciturn. Perhaps I am, because I have to open my mouth so often to laugh.

I go through life with an impassive expression, from time to time permitting myself a gentle smile, and I often wonder whether I have ever laughed. I think not. My brothers and sisters have always known me for a serious boy.

So I laugh in many different ways, but my own laughter I have never heard.

*Translated by Leila Vennewitz*

PAULA FOX

# News from the World

NOTHING MUCH used to happen around here. In summer, there were more car accidents and fires and scandals. Dying went on year round, and in our village by the sea, most people breathed their last in the early hours of the morning. I'd heard that was so elsewhere.

There was no sound from the world in winter. The snow and the sea closed us in. We had our own news. But in June, in the kitchens of the houses where we worked, we heard the babble of other places. In time, I learned that the people who came here expected something more than they could find in stories of soldiers burning villages far away, or of thieves stealing governments, or of the killing of politicians.

During the long evenings, we villagers went to the beach and collected the things they had thrown away or lost, bottles and change, rings and toys, and as we sifted through the sand, we found traces of their secret lives, their vices and wishes.

Last June, a vast pool of oil formed a mile from our shore. The summer people stood in groups on the edge of the sea; their faces flamed in the sunset as though they were seeing paradise.

That same June, I fell in love with an old man. I cleaned his kitchen, did his shopping, sniffed at his tubes of paint, touched his damp canvases, ironed his fine linen shirts and, each morning, straightened his scarcely rumpled bed.

When, at an early hour, he came to drink the coffee I had made him, I felt as though my eyes had fallen out of my head, and in their sockets, there was only light.

He was a thin old man, as limber as a youth. His hair was nearly white but his beard was black. His clear, pale voice flowed like a brook over a shallow bed. His slight stammer assured me he was shy despite the paintings of naked men and women that hung in the room where he painted. He spoke to me only of the weather.

"Is it a good morning?" he would ask, as though he weren't standing right in it.

"There's a mist, but it will be gone in an hour," I might say.

"A thick mist? A sea mist?" he would press.

"A ground mist," I'd reply, "just over the dunes and already lifting."

To describe him is to say nothing of what stirred me. It would be as foolish as to say the sky is blue and the sand is yellow. Words are nets through which all truth escapes.

One morning at the end of July, as I was passing by his chair, he placed his hands directly on my buttocks. I stood like a statue in the hollow center of which an animal flutters and scrabbles frantically to escape. When I got home that day, my children looked like strangers, and my husband's name tasted in my mouth like metal.

All through August, while I cleaned his little house behind the dunes, we spoke of mist, fog, wind, heat and rain. But when he rested his hands on various parts of my body, I waited in silence until he went back to his coffee. During those moments, I burned with a flame that was both hot and cold.

When I thought of the winter months, when the old man would be gone, the little house shuttered against the freezing wind, I knew what it would be like to feel death creeping around my feet.

I began to read the newspapers from the city which you could only buy in my village during the three months of summer, but what I read was weak and sickly. It had not the power to turn me from this terrible love that had struck me down and crushed me in my fortieth year. I longed only to submit to the torment of that light which filled my head those mornings I watched him walk toward me with his youth's light step across the rag rug of the parlor.

"Good morning," we each said, and it was as though my heart burst loose from its nest of blood and flew like a bird toward the sky.

All summer, the pool of oil had moved closer and closer to the shore. Men came in boats and tried to bait it as though it was a wild beast. There were always fires on the beach at night, and around them people sang and embraced, their faces turned away from the dark sea.

"Will you accompany me to the shore?" the old man asked me one noon, just as I had tucked my apron away in a paper sack. We sat on the sand among the crowd who called out to each other as they pulled thick, oily strands of devil's apron from the water.

We sat, each with our arms around our knees; our shoulders touched. Mixed with the smell of salt was his own fragrance, linseed oil and laundered linen, and the green pine soap I bought for him at the store.

Dying birds lay around our feet, and an arm's length away was a sand shark whose jaw opened and slowly stiffened.

He rose to his feet so lightly, I thought he had only sighed. Before I could cry out, he was waist high in the oil and water, flinging seabirds out upon the beach, while all around people laughed and clapped their hands.

I reached him as he fell. I carried him through the crowd whose faces had gone cold and angry.

I undressed him in the kitchen. In the narrow tub that stood on claw feet, I bathed him in warm water. I washed the oil from the wings of his hair and rinsed away every drop of it from the most tender and private parts of his body. Then I dried him and dressed him in fresh clothes I had ironed myself, and I tied the laces of his shoes and combed his damp beard.

In the kitchen, I fed him whiskey and coffee. At last the color came back to his cheeks.

He wanted me, he said, to leave the village and my children and my husband, to return with him to the city he came from. He said that there, each night, we would hear music in a different place.

I listened to him for an hour, hearing parts of his voice I'd not heard before. While he spoke, he often gripped his fine old hands together as though he were pressing something out of himself. He said there was no future for me in the village.

"You live on the edge of things," he said.

When he had finished, he lay back against the chair, his eyelids fluttering. I stood up. I folded my apron and said I wouldn't go with him although I loved him better than my village or his city or anything that walked or flew or crawled.

This winter I have often gone to look at the house where he lived. It is blowing away, a board here, a shingle there.

Inside the scarf which I wrap around my throat and jaw, I can taste my own moist breath. Inside the sleeves of my coat, where I've drawn them against the cold, my hands form cups to hold the balls of his feet, the joints of his kneecaps, the small cheeks of his behind, the angel's wings of his narrow shoulder blades.

No one will come back this summer to his house or any other house. Our beach is black with oil. Our birds are dead or gone. The fish lie frozen beneath the ooze. The dune grass cannot grow. Officials come every week and note down what news they can find in the tides of black muck. They speak only among themselves in the dunes, the wind pressing their coat collars against their clean-shaven jaws.

It is too late for reports. We are starving here in our village. At last, we are at the center.

## MARIA LUISE KASCHNITZ

# Going to Jerusalem

LAST YEAR IN MAY a mysterious disease spread throughout our town. In the months to follow it attacked the greater part of the population. The doctors knew nothing about the causes and the nature of this disease. They treated the symptoms—the patients' general debility and unusual restlessness—with the standard fortifying or subduing remedies. It was said they were waiting for the first patient to die so that they could dissect him and use the findings to continue their research. In the meantime, though they themselves were sick by now, they tried to reassure their patients who were not bedridden. In fact, most of the patients came to their waiting rooms almost daily for fear of missing a newly discovered cure or any other new development. They assured them that in spite of their extreme weakness and nervous trembling, their vital organs were not affected and that there was no cause for alarm. And as long as the doctors kept seeing them, the patients were completely convinced that they were right. Their dispositions improved and they were even able to make jokes. But this cheerfulness was short-lived. As soon as they went out into the street and saw all the frightened faces nervously twitching they fell back into their former gloom and fear.

In the last few days of summer the morale in our town was already quite low. No one had been allowed to leave the city during those summer months because of the very real possibility of contagion and this had left us all in an extremely depressed state. Many of us had imagined that we need only have left the city for a vacation in order to get well—just as a terminally ill patient desperately wants to leave his bed because he believes that he will be truly tormented there and only there. The first death, which was generally regarded as the last form of salvation, had not occurred yet, and we were beginning to watch each other closely, on the lookout for the shadow of death in the faces of even our most beloved friends.

The strange events I am about to relate took place on three consecutive days in the month of October, in the waiting room of my doctor, who was widely reputed for his extreme patience and whose waiting room was always crowded. On the first day all of the chairs had already been taken by nine o'clock, and there were many people standing between them. It was cold and damp outside. A light was burning in the vestibule which served as an additional waiting room; winter coats were clinging to each other on the coat racks while their owners were crouched down next to each other in morose silence. All of a sudden a man began to tell a story. No one wanted to listen to him—after all, we weren't in the Orient—and how could people in our situation still care about stories anyway? The man was leaning against the wall way in the back of the room and took no notice of our angry coughing; his voice, which had sounded just as dull and weak as ours at first, grew increasingly stronger as he continued to talk. This aroused astonishment and then anger. I turned around to look at him; he was pale just as we all were, of medium height, middle-aged and shabbily dressed. He had bright, inquisitive eyes like those of a child. The story he was telling was repulsive. It was the story of a man who had been eaten alive by rats in a prison and who was thinking about all sorts of equally horrible experiences while this was happening. However, the defiant perseverance with which the storyteller presented these atrocities had us all listening to him in the end—attentively, no, even eagerly.

The following day at about the same time most of the same people as the day before were in the waiting room, since the doctor had closed his office early. The stranger was there as well and was leaning against the same place on the panelled wall as he had the day before. When it looked as if he were about to begin another story, he immediately had an attentive audience—an audience that angrily hissed at each newcomer entering the room as if they were in the theater or in a concert hall. However, it soon turned out that the stranger had no intention of telling a story this time, either because he was too tired or too listless. He said one word, was silent for a long time, said another word and stopped again, and so on and so forth. It was not particularly entertaining since these words had no connection with each other and were not even special words; in short, it was a sort of hodgepodge. It seems incomprehensible why we listened to him so attentively and why every patient called into the doctor's office only went hesitatingly, almost against his will. It was probably because each individually spoken word evoked certain memories or hopes within us. Somehow each word seemed to hang in empty space, large and heavy.

On the following day the mood in the waiting room was cheerful, one could almost say it was gay. The stranger had come up with a game for us to play and had already begun to give us instructions. Many chairs were needed for the game and some were taken out of the doctor's dining room. I suddenly remembered, wasn't there supposed to be a piano, too, with someone playing "I'm Going to Jerusalem"; then the player suddenly stops and everyone has to find a seat, but there aren't enough for everyone; one chair is missing. Crazy, I thought, a game like this in a doctor's waiting room. What are we anyway, children? But I said nothing; I got in line and began circling the chairs along with everyone else. There was no piano. The stranger was drumming out a beat on a gong with his fingers. The gong was probably part of the doctor's dining room set. The stranger was beating out an entrancing but terrifying rhythm. We moved forward, giggling, whispering and then becoming silent, faster and faster, tripping, shuffling along, always expecting the drumming to stop. When it finally did, we rushed for the chairs, no longer playfully, but filled with fear and anger as if it were of the utmost importance—a matter of life and death—to get a seat. And then we were suddenly all sitting; no one was standing. There was no chair missing after all—but why? Because the stranger had fallen down, because he was lying sprawled out on the floor next to the door, dead.

Almost a year has passed since the day we played that childish game in the doctor's waiting room. The disease is as good as cured; even the most difficult cases have shown signs of improvement. It's possible, but no one knows for sure, that our town was saved by the death of the first victim, that very same storyteller and word-sayer. It's also possible that at precisely that time a cure for the mysterious disease had been discovered somewhere else, in a completely different country, in America or in Australia; in any case, a lot of research has been done on it. But even if that is true, I shall continue to think of that peculiar stranger for a long time to come. I will try to reconstruct his unpleasant story; sometimes I catch myself beating out the fascinating rhythm of his drumming with my fingers on a table. I will try to recall and write down the words he had said between the long periods of silence. Blackberry—bush—rain—ice flower—midnight . . . is it possible that it really wasn't anything else?

*Translated by Claudia Stoeffler*

# LUISA VALENZUELA

## The Censors

POOR JUAN! One day they caught him with his guard down before he could even realize that what he had taken as a stroke of luck was really one of fate's dirty tricks. These things happen the minute you're careless and you let down your guard, as one often does. Juancito let happiness—a feeling you can't trust—get the better of him when he received from a confidential source Mariana's new address in Paris and he knew that she hadn't forgotten him. Without thinking twice, he sat down at his table and wrote her a letter. *The* letter that keeps his mind off his job during the day and won't let him sleep at night (what had he scrawled, what had he put on that sheet of paper he sent to Mariana?).

Juan knows there won't be a problem with the letter's contents, that it's irreproachable, harmless. But what about the rest? He knows that they examine, sniff, feel, and read between the lines of each and every letter, and check it tiniest comma and most accidental stain. He knows that all letters pass from hand to hand and go through all sorts of tests in the huge censorship offices and that, in the end, very few continue on their way. Usually it takes months, even years, if there aren't any snags; all this time the freedom, maybe even the life, of both sender and receiver is in jeopardy. And that's why Juan's so down in the dumps: thinking that something might happen to Mariana because of his letters. Of all people, Mariana, who must finally feel safe there where she always dreamed she'd live. But he knows that the *Censor's Secret Command* operates all over the world and cashes in on the discount in air rates; there's nothing to stop them from going as far as that hidden Paris neighborhood, kidnapping Mariana, and returning to their cozy homes, certain of having fulfilled their noble mission.

Well, you've got to beat them to the punch, do what everyone tries to do: sabotage the machinery, throw sand in its gears, get to the bottom of the problem so as to stop it.

This was Juan's sound plan when he, like many others, applied for a censor's job—not because he had a calling or needed a job: no, he applied simply to intercept his own letter, a consoling but unoriginal idea. He was hired immediately, for each day more and more censors are needed and no one would bother to check on his references.

Ulterior motives couldn't be overlooked by the *Censorship Divison,* but they needn't be too strict with those who applied. They knew how hard it would be for those poor guys to find the letter they wanted and even if they did, what's a letter or two when the new censor would snap up so many others? That's how Juan managed to join the *Post Office's Censorship Division,* with a certain goal in mind.

The building had a festive air on the outside which contrasted with its inner staidness. Little by little, Juan was absorbed by his job and he felt at peace since he was doing everything he could to get his letter for Mariana. He didn't even worry when, in his first month, he was sent to *Section K* where envelopes are very carefully screened for explosives.

It's true that on the third day, a fellow worker had his right hand blown off by a letter, but the division chief claimed it was sheer negligence on the victim's part. Juan and the other employees were allowed to go back to their work, albeit feeling less secure. After work, one of them tried to organize a strike to demand higher wages for unhealthy work, but Juan didn't join in; after thinking it over, he reported him to his superiors and thus got promoted.

You don't form a habit by doing something once, he told himself as he left his boss's office. And when he was transferred to *Section J*, where letters are carefully checked for poison dust, he felt he had climbed a rung in the ladder.

By working hard, he quickly reached *Section E* where the work was more interesting, for he could now read and analyze the letters' contents. Here he could even hope to get hold of his letter which, judging by the time that had elapsed, had gone through the other sections and was probably floating around in this one.

Soon his work became so absorbing that his noble mission blurred in his mind. Day after day he crossed out whole paragraphs in red ink, pitilessly chucking many letters into the censored basket. These were horrible days when he was shocked by the subtle and conniving ways employed by people to pass on subversive messages; his instincts were so sharp that he found behind a simple "the weather's unsettled" or "prices continue to soar" the wavering hand of someone secretly scheming to overthrow the Government.

His zeal brought him swift promotion. We don't know if this made him happy. Very few letters reached him in *Section B*—only a handful passed the other hurdles—so he read them over and over again, passed them under a magnifying glass, searched for microprint with an electronic microscope, and tuned his sense of smell so that he was beat by the time he made it home. He'd barely manage to warm up his soup, eat some fruit, and fall into bed, satisfied with having done his duty. Only his darling mother worried, but she couldn't get him back on the right road. She'd say, though it wasn't always true: Lola called, she's at the bar with the girls, they miss you, they're waiting for you. Or else she'd leave a bottle of red wine on the table. But Juan wouldn't overdo it: any distraction could make him lose his edge and the perfect censor had to be alert, keen, attentive, and sharp to nab cheats. He had a truly patriotic task, both self-denying and uplifting.

His basket for censored letters became the best fed as well as the most cunning basket in the whole *Censorship Division*. He was about to congratulate himself for having finally discovered his true mission, when his letter to Mariana reached his hands. Naturally, he censored it without regret. And just as naturally, he couldn't stop them from executing him the following morning, another victim of his devotion to his work.

*Translated by David Unger*

*Copyright Notices and Acknowledgements*

"Eveline." From THE DUBLINERS by James Joyce. Copyright © 1967 by the Estate of James Joyce. Reprinted by permission of Viking Penguin, Inc., and by permission of Jonathan Cape Ltd.

"First Sorrow" and "The Hunter Gracchus." From THE COMPLETE STORIES by Franz Kafka. Copyright © 1946, 1947, 1948, 1949, 1954, 1958, 1971 by Schocken Books, Inc. Reprinted by permission of Schocken Books, Inc.

"Going to Jerusalem" by Maria Luise Kaschnitz. Translation by Claudia Stoessler.

"A Little Legend of the Dance." From THE PEOPLE OF SELDWYLA AND SEVEN LEGENDS by Gottfried Keller. Copyright © 1929 by J.M. Dent Ltd. Reprinted by permission of J.M. Dent Ltd.

"The Beggarwoman of Locarno." From THE MARQUISE OF O & OTHER STORIES by Heinrich von Kleist, translation by Martin Greenberg (Criterion Books). Introduction and English translation of the stories copyright © 1960 by Martin Greenberg. Reprinted by permission of Harper & Row, Publishers, Inc.

"Joy and the Law" by Giuseppe di Lampedusa. Reprinted by permission of Granada Publishing Ltd., and by permission of Paul Elek Ltd.

"A Sick Collier" by D.H. Lawrence, from THE COMPLETE SHORT STORIES OF D. H. LAWRENCE. Copyright © 1933 by the Estate of D.H. Lawrence; copyright renewed 1961 by Angelo Ravagli and C.M. Weekley, Executors of the Estate of Frieda Lawrence Ravagli. Reprinted by permission of Viking Penguin, Inc., and by permission of Laurence Pollinger Ltd.

"Homage for Isaac Babel." From A MAN AND TWO WOMEN by Doris Lessing. Copyright © 1958, 1962, 1963 by Doris Lessing. Reprinted by permission of Simon & Schuster. Also reprinted by permission of Curtis Brown Ltd.

"Bitterness for Three Sleepwalkers." From INNOCENT ERENDIRA AND OTHER STORIES by Gabriel García Márquez. English translation copyright © 1978 by Harper & Row, Publishers, Inc. Reprinted by permission of Harper &

Row, Publishers, Inc. Also reprinted by permission of Jonathan Cape Ltd.

"An Old Man." From MAUPASSANT: SELECTED SHORT STORIES by Guy de Maupassant, translated by Roger Colet. Copyright © 1971 by Roger Colet. Reprinted by permission of Penguin Books Ltd.

"Swaddling Clothes." From DEATH IN MIDSUMMER AND OTHER STORIES by Yukio Mishima. Copyright © 1966 by New Directions Publishing Corp. Reprinted by permission of New Directions Publishing Corp. Also reprinted by permission of Laurence Pollinger Ltd.

"The Eclipse." From COMPLETE WORKS AND OTHER STORIES by Augusto Monterroso. Copyright © by Augusto Monterroso. Reprinted by permission of Augusto Monterroso.

"Wants." From ENORMOUS CHANGES AT THE LAST MINUTE by Grace Paley. Copyright © 1971, 1974 by Grace Paley. Reprinted by permission of Farrar, Straus & Giroux.

"The Blue Bouquet." From EAGLE OR SUN? by Octavio Paz. Copyright © 1969, 1970, 1975, 1976 by Octavio Paz and Eliot Weinberger. Reprinted by permission of New Directions Publishing Corp.

"If Not Higher" by I. L. Peretz, from A TREASURY OF YIDDISH STORIES, eds. Irving Howe and Eliezer Greenberg, translated by Marie Syrkin. Copyright © 1953, 1954 by Viking Press. Copyright © 1981, 1982 by Isaac B. Singer. Reprinted by permission of Viking Penguin, Inc.

"The Soft Touch of Grass" by Luigi Pirandello, from SHORT STORIES BY PIRANDELLO, translated by Lily Duplaix. Copyright © 1959 by Gli Eredi Luigi Pirandello. Reprinted by permission of Simon & Schuster.

"Magic." From FLOWERING JUDAS AND OTHER STORIES by Katherine Anne Porter. Copyright © 1930, 1958 by Katherine Anne Porter. Reprinted by permission of Harcourt Brace Jovanovich, Inc., and by permission of Jonathan Cape Ltd.

"The Third Bank of the River" by João Guimaraes Rosa, from MODERN BRAZILIAN SHORT STORIES, edited and translated by William L. Grossman. Copyright © 1967 by the Regents of the University of California. Reprinted by permission of the University of California Press.

"In the Night." From KOLYMA TALES by Varlam Shalamov, translated by John Glad. Copyright © 1980 by John Glad. Reprinted by permission of W.W. Norton, Inc.

"If Grant Had Been Drinking at Appomattox." From THE MIDDLE AGED MAN ON THE FLYING TRAPEZE by James Thurber. Copyright © 1950 by James Thurber. Copyright © 1963 by Helen W. Thurber and Rosemary T. Sauers. Reprinted by permission of Helen W. Thurber. Also reprinted by permission of Hamish Hamilton Ltd.

"The Three Hermits." From TWENTY-THREE TALES by Leo Tolstoy, translated by Louise and Aylmer Maude (World Classics, 1906). Reprinted by permission of Oxford University Press.

"The Censors" by Luisa Valenzuela. Copyright © by Luisa Valenzuela. Reprinted by permission of Luisa Valenzuela.

"The Wolf" by Giovanni Verga. Reprinted by permission of Granada Publishing Ltd., and by permission of Paul Elek Ltd.

"My Father Sits in the Dark." From MY FATHER SITS IN THE DARK AND OTHER STORIES by Jerome Weidman. Copyright © 1934 and copyright renewed 1962 by Jerome Weidman. Reprinted by permission of Random House, Inc., and by permission of Brandt & Brandt, Inc.

"The Use of Force." From THE FARMER'S DAUGHTER: COLLECTED SHORT STORIES by William Carlos Williams. Copyright © 1938 by William Carlos Williams. Reprinted by permission of New Directions Publishing Corp.

"The Bathhouse." From SCENES FROM THE BATHHOUSE AND OTHER STORIES OF COMMUNIST RUSSIA by Mikhail Zoshchenko, translated by Sidney Monas. Copyright © 1961 by The University of Michigan Press, Ann Arbor. Reprinted by permission of The University of Michigan Press.

# ABOUT THE AUTHORS

LEO TOLSTOY (1828–1910), the great Russian novelist, wrote *Anna Karenina* and *War and Peace*. Late in his life, he espoused a radical, pacifist Christianity which brought him many followers.

HEINRICH VON KLEIST (1778–1811), an important figure in the German Romantic movement, was a journalist, editor, publisher and author of eight plays and eight stories. He died at age 33 in a suicide pact.

GOTTFRIED KELLER (1819–1890) was born in Zurich and studied in Germany. He returned to Switzerland and became a Zurich city official and a prolific author of poems, novels and stories.

ANTON CHEKHOV (1860–1904), born in Taganrog, Russia, was a medical student in Moscow when his first stories were published. His plays (*The Seagull, The Cherry Orchard*) are classics of modern drama. Of his stories, he once said, "I can speak briefly on long subjects."

GIOVANNI VERGA (1840–1922), though born into the landed gentry, spent most of his writing career depicting the lives of the peasantry of his native Sicily. A leading exponent of *verismo,* a kind of realism, he wrote *Cavalleria rusticana,* on which the opera is based, and *The House by the Medlar Tree.*

STEPHEN CRANE (1871–1900) was born in New Jersey and raised in upstate New York. As a New York City reporter, he wrote his novel *Maggie: A Girl of the Streets,* but could not find a publisher for it. Without any first-hand knowledge of war, he wrote *The Red Badge of Courage,* which made him famous. He later reported on combat in Greece and Cuba.

GUY DE MAUPASSANT, born in Normandy in 1850, was a civil servant until writing began to make him a wealthy man. Under the guidance of Flaubert, he mastered the art of the short story and produced sixteen volumes of stories before his early death in 1893.

JOÃO GUIMARÃES ROSA (1908–1967) was born in Minas Gerais, Brazil. After medical training, he practiced in a rural area where he also collected the folk tales of the region. He served Brazil as a diplomat. His most famous novel appears in English as *The Devil to Pay in the Backlands.*

SHOLOM ALEICHEM was the pen name of Sholom Rabinowitz, born in Russia in 1859. The most popular of all Yiddish writers, this great humorist left Russia after the 1905 pogrom in Kiev, and died in the U.S. in 1916.

ISAAC LEIB PERETZ (1851–1915) was a major architect of modern Yiddish literature. He practiced law for several years before devoting himself to writing and to Jewish community affairs in Warsaw. There he was at the center of cultural and political ferment among the East European Jews.

JAMES JOYCE (1882–1941) left his native Dublin in 1904 for Trieste. There he taught English, wrote *A Portrait of the Artist as a Young Man,* and started *Ulysses,* which he finished in Paris in 1922. His stories are collected in *Dubliners.*

DAVID HERBERT LAWRENCE was born in Nottingham, England in 1885, the son of a coal miner. He wrote ten novels, including *Sons and Lovers, The Rainbow,* and *Women in Love,* and many volumes of poetry, stories and criticism. He lived in Europe, Australia and Mexico, and died in France in 1930.

LUIGI PIRANDELLO (1867–1936), born in Sicily, wrote short stories (collected as *Stories for a Year*) before he turned to the theater. A director and producer as well as playwright, he is best known for his play, *Six Characters in Search of an Author.* He received the Nobel Prize in 1934.

FRANZ KAFKA (1883–1924) was a Czech Jew who wrote in German. One of this century's most powerful and disturbing writers, he made his living as an official in a government insurance bureau. His novels are: *The Trial, The Castle* and *Amerika.*

SHERWOOD ANDERSON (1876–1941) was born in Ohio and drifted through a series of jobs until, at the age of 40, he published his first novel. It was his third book, the series of stories called *Winesburg, Ohio,* which made his reputation as a chronicler of small-town life.

ERNEST HEMINGWAY, born in Illinois in 1898, was a reporter for a Kansas City newspaper, then went to France as a volunteer ambulance driver in World War I. As an expatriate in post-war Paris, he first achieved success with the stories in *In Our Time.* His novels include *The Sun Also Rises* and *A Farewell to Arms.* He committed suicide in 1961.

GIUSEPPE TOMASI DI LAMPEDUSA (1896–1957) was a Sicilian aristocrat whose single novel, *The Leopard,* was not begun until the author was 60. It was published posthumously, to great acclaim, in 1958.

KATHERINE ANNE PORTER was born in Indian Creek, Texas, in 1890. She worked as a journalist and screen writer while writing her tense, finely crafted stories and novellas. Her books include *Flowering Judas* and *Pale Horse, Pale Rider.* She died in 1980.

ISAAC BABEL was born in Odessa in 1894. He served in the Red Army during its campaign in Poland in 1920, an experience which produced the stories in *Red Cavalry.* Though an honored Soviet writer, he grew disenchanted with the regime and was finally arrested in 1937. He presumably died in a concentration camp in 1939 or 1940.

MIKHAIL ZOSHCHENKO (1895–1958) was born in the Ukraine and fought in the Russian Civil War. He published a number of witty, ironic stories in Moscow in the 1920s and '30s. After being condemned for "ideological errors" in 1946, he spent his last years writing biographies.

WILLIAM CARLOS WILLIAMS (1883–1963), who worked as a New Jersey physician, was an important American poet. His stories are collected in *The Farmers' Daughters.* His poems include *Paterson* and *Pictures from Breughel.*

YUKIO MISHIMA, born in Tokyo in 1925, was one of Japan's great modern novelists and playwrights, the author of *Confessions of a Mask* and *Sun and Steel.* His belief in restoring Japan's martial traditions led to his public ritual suicide in 1970.

JAMES THURBER was born in Ohio in 1894. His cartoons, stories and sketches appeared in the *New Yorker* magazine for many years. His collections include *The Owl in the Attic* and *The Thurber Carnival.* He died in 1961.

DORIS LESSING (born 1919) grew up in Southern Rhodesia (now Zimbabwe), where her first novels are set. She has lived in England since 1949. Her books include *The Golden Notebook, The Four-Gated City,* and *Stories.*

JORGE LUIS BORGES was born in Buenos Aires in 1899 and educated in Europe. He is a distinguished poet and critic, and was director of the National Library of Argentina. His stories are collected in *Ficciones, The Aleph,* and *Dr. Brodie's Report.*

VARLAM SHALAMOV'S (circa 1907–1/17/82) stories of prison camp life have circulated privately in the Soviet Union. They were published in the West as *Kolyma Tales.*

OCTAVIO PAZ (born 1914) is an eminent Mexican poet and critic. He entered the diplomatic service in 1945 and was Mexico's ambassador to India from 1962 to 1968. His books include *The Labyrinth of Solitude* and *Eagle or Sun?*

JEROME WEIDMAN, born in New York City in 1913, is the author of many novels, including *I Can Get It For You Wholesale* and *Fourth Street East.* He has also written plays and musicals.

GRACE PALEY was born in 1922 and has lived in New York City all her life. She has published poems and two volumes of stories, *The Little Disturbances of Man* and *Enormous Changes at the Last Minute.*

GABRIEL GARCÍA MÁRQUEZ won the 1982 Nobel Prize for Literature. Born in Aracataca, Colombia in 1928, he is the author of *One Hundred Years of Solitude* and *The Autumn of the Patriarch.*

AUGUSTO MONTERROSO was born in Guatemala in 1921. He has lived in Mexico since 1944, where he has published two volumes of stories and a book of fables, published in English as *The Black Sheep.*

HEINRICH BÖLL, born in Cologne in 1917, is one of Germany's most prominent post-war writers. His novels include *The Clown, Billiards at Half-Past Nine,* and *Group Portrait with Lady.* He received the Nobel Prize in 1972.

PAULA FOX was born in New York City in 1923. She has published several novels including *Desperate Characters* and *The Widow's Children,* and is also a well-known author of children's books.

MARIA LUISE KASCHNITZ was born in Karlsruhe, Germany, in 1901. Since 1948, she has published several volumes of poetry and a book of stories, *Lange Schatten.*

LUISA VALENZUELA, born in Argentina in 1938, is the author of *Clara: 13 Short Stories and a Novel,* and two other collections.

*A note about the editors*

IRVING and ILANA HOWE live in Manhattan and trade stories short, long, and longer. His books include *World of Our Fathers, Politics and the Novel, Thomas Hardy, Steady Work, William Faulkner,* and *The Portable Kipling.*